FACING THE FUTURE

Facing the Future

LEFT BEHIND™

>THE KIDS<

Jerry B. Jenkins

Tim LaHaye

TYNDALE
KIDS

TYNDALE HOUSE PUBLISHERS, INC.
WHEATON, ILLINOIS

Visit Tyndale's exciting Web site at www.tyndale.com

Discover the latest Left Behind news at www.leftbehind.com

Left Behind is a trademark of Tyndale House Publishers, Inc.

Published in association with the literary agency of Alive Communications, Inc., 1465 Kelly Johnson Blvd., Suite 320, Colorado Springs, CO 80920.

Designed by Brian Eterno
Edited by Rick Blanchette

ISBN 0-8423-2196-9

Printed in the United States of America

04   03   02   01   00   99
12   11   10   9

To Jamie, Jeremy, and Jason

CONTENTS

What's Gone On Before

JUDD Thompson Jr. and the other three kids living in his house had been involved in the adventure of a lifetime. But it wasn't something they would have chosen.

They had been horrifyingly left alone a few weeks before when their families disappeared in the global vanishings—or, in the case of Ryan Daley, when his parents had been killed in accidents related to the disappearances.

Judd was the oldest at sixteen, the only one who could drive. His father, mother, and younger brother and sister had disappeared in the middle of the night.

Vicki Byrne, fourteen, had lost her parents and her little sister, who had vanished right out of their trailer home. Her brother, who had moved to Michigan, had also disappeared.

Lionel Washington, thirteen, had lost his

parents, an older sister, and two younger siblings. His uncle, André Dupree, had been left behind too, but his recent murder had led to the situation in which the four now found themselves.

They had stumbled onto each other and a young pastor at a local church. The older three of the four had been church kids and knew immediately that the disappearances meant only one thing: What they had heard about in church, what their parents had warned them about for years, had come true. Jesus Christ had returned to snatch away his church, his true believers, in the twinkling of an eye. All over the world, millions had disappeared right out of their clothes, leaving behind everything but flesh and blood and bone.

Ryan, twelve, had had little idea what had happened. All he knew was that he was suddenly an orphan. His father had died in a plane crash when the pilot had disappeared. His mother was killed in a gas-main explosion during the chaos that followed the vanishings.

Ryan had been the last of the four to see the truth and the last to make the decision to believe in Christ, to trust him for forgiveness of sin and to assure himself that he would go to be with God when he died.

Vicki's trailer had burned to the ground. Lionel's home had been invaded and taken over by his uncle's "friends." Ryan was afraid to stay alone in his own house, especially after it had been burglarized. So, the four new Christians had settled into Judd Thompson's huge home in the Chicago suburb of Mount Prospect, Illinois. They attended New Hope Village Church and sat under the teaching of Bruce Barnes. While dealing with their grief and fear over the loss of their families, they were also striving to learn as much as they could about what had happened and what was to come.

Bruce Barnes had been that rare full-time Christian worker, on the pastoral staff, who himself had been left behind. He had lost his wife and small children to the vanishings. He knew immediately that he had never been a true believer and quickly turned his life over to God. In his grief and remorse he became an outspoken witness for Christ, telling everyone who would listen that they needed to come to God.

He also taught that the Rapture (Christ's snatching away of the church) was not the beginning of the seven-year tribulation the Bible predicted, where the earth and its inhabitants would suffer tremendous devastation and loss. No, he said, prophecy indicated that a great leader would arise, the Antichrist, the great enemy of God. He would make a pact with Israel, and the day that was signed would signal the beginning of the seven years.

The kids left behind were fascinated by what Bruce taught, and they wanted to be on the lookout for the Antichrist. He was, Bruce said, a great deceiver who would appear to be an attractive and articulate peacemaker and would fool many. They didn't want to be fooled. They wanted to stand and fight. And they wanted others to come to Christ too.

But in the meantime, just surviving had become a chore. Lionel's uncle André had appeared to have committed suicide after realizing he had been left behind. But when Lionel went to identify the body, it wasn't André's!

LeRoy Banks, leader of the small band that had taken over Lionel's house, had murdered an enemy and forced André to make it appear the body was his own. André first called Lionel's answering machine and left a long, rambling, pitiful message about how he was going to do away with himself. Then the deed was done in André's apartment, and the victim—about André's size—wore André's clothes and jewelry and carried his identification.

When the body turned out to be someone else, Lionel and his new friends set about trying to find André. But when LeRoy found out that Lionel had discovered the truth about the fake suicide, he was afraid Lionel or André would reveal the truth to the police. He sent André into hiding, putting him in the apartment of another friend, Cornelius Grey.

Lionel made Cornelius Grey's sister, Talia, take him there to see his uncle. When LeRoy found out, he was sure they were conspiring to expose his murder to the police. Just after Talia and then Lionel had left André, LeRoy charged into Cornelius Grey's apartment, shot André, and set the place afire.

Judd, who had been nearby waiting for Lionel, raced into the burning building and helped Lionel drag his uncle out. But it was too late. LeRoy had murdered yet again. Now Lionel was in danger from LeRoy, who would have to keep killing to be sure no one was alive who knew what he had done.

Judd enlisted the aid of Chicago police sergeant Tom Fogarty and came up with a plan to lure in LeRoy and his friend, Cornelius ("Connie") Grey. Sergeant Fogarty set up a phony legal office in Chicago, and Vicki Byrne called Cornelius to tell him that insurance money might be due him because of the fire in his apartment.

The plan was to call LeRoy from Ryan's house, just in case he grew suspicious and tried to trace the call. Ryan, Lionel, and Judd sat quietly while Vicki dialed. She threw on a very adult-sounding voice. Cornelius Grey answered the phone.

"Mr. Grey, this is Maria Diablo from the law offices of Thomas Fogarty in Chicago. Mr. Fogarty is representing the insurance company handling the settlements in the destruction by fire of your apartment building last week."

"Yeah, what do we get?"

"Well, sir, I'm not at liberty to discuss the amount over the phone, but I can tell you it is substantial. Unfortunately, the payout must go to the payer of the rent over the last several months, and our records indicate that it has not been you."

"No, the rent's been paid lately by a friend of mine, helpin' me out. Name is LeRoy Banks."

"Would I be able to speak to him?"

"Sure!"

Judd and the others heard Cornelius Grey quickly fill in LeRoy on their huge stroke of luck. "Let me have that phone," LeRoy said, clearly doubtful.

"Who is this?" he demanded.

Vicki went through the same routine with him, in its entirety, just the way Judd had scripted it. Rather than let LeRoy build on his doubts, she made the prize a little harder to get.

"Of course, sir, we would not be able to issue a check of this magnitude unless you were able to prove to us that you are the same LeRoy Banks who has been paying the rent on Cornelius Grey's apartment."

"Oh, I'll be able to prove it all right. What time did you say Mr. Fogarty could see me?"

On the way back to Judd's house, Lionel and Ryan congratulated Judd for his idea and Vicki for her performance. When they arrived, Judd prepared to call Sergeant Fogarty to fill him in on how things had gone. Not only did he want to tell Fogarty when to expect to see LeRoy Banks and Cornelius Grey, but he also wanted to beg to be there himself to see the big arrest. It was only fair that Vicki be allowed there too, but he couldn't imagine the Chicago Police Department allowing civilians close to what could become a dangerous situation.

Still, he would ask. He wanted above anything to see the look on LeRoy's face when
he found out he was not getting a check but
rather getting arrested for murder. When
Judd reached for the phone, however, it rang.

"Are you watching channel nine?" Bruce
Barnes asked Judd.

"No, we're in the middle of—"

"Turn on nine," Bruce insisted. "I've got a
hunch the guy they're interviewing could be
the one we're supposed to watch out for."

"You mean the Antichrist?" Judd asked,
grabbing the remote control. He wanted to
tell Bruce the story of the sting, but that
would have to wait until he talked to Fogarty.

He thanked Bruce and turned on the television, watching in fascination. "You'd better
call the sergeant," Vicki suggested.

"Yeah!" he said, turning down the volume
and dialing the number.

Fogarty was ecstatic, and he wasn't closed
to the idea of Judd and Vicki being there
when it all happened. "We have a one-way
mirror at the back where my backups will be.
That's where they'll come from to surprise
these two when I give the signal. I think if
you two agree to stay there until it's all over,
you could have a great view and stay safe. It'd
be too risky to have your young friend there,
and we don't want the murder victim's

nephew in the neighborhood at all that day, just in case."

"But Vicki and I can come, really?"

"Sure. Just be sure you're an hour early and park far away."

Judd couldn't wait. As he hung up he looked at his watch and decided he and Vicki would have to leave within the hour to be downtown in time to be in place. He turned up the TV and watched more of the interview with the man Bruce now suspected could be the Antichrist.

Boy, would he and Bruce have a lot to talk about the next time they got together!

ONE

The Ride

JUDD felt a tingle down his spine as he and Vicki got in the car. He'd had enough excitement for a lifetime the last couple of weeks, but he had never been involved in anything like this. He had been a rebel, a difficult, stubborn, self-centered teen. Lying to his parents and running with the wrong crowd had been the extent of his adventure—at least until the Rapture.

His world had been turned upside down. Meeting three other instant orphans, having them move in, and all four of them coming to Christ within a few days made his previous life seem eons ago. Was it possible that just a few weeks ago he thought he knew everything there was to know about just about everything? Now, strange as it seemed, he knew he was more mature and grown-up than ever, mostly because he realized how little he knew about anything.

Everything important to him before now seemed childish and stupid. What he cared about now was God. People. Truth. Justice. Survival. In a way, he missed the carefree youth he had been squandering by playing the tough guy. Rascal though he was, his parents were always there to bail him out. And while they may have wondered what would ever become of him, he knew down deep they would have even forgiven him for stealing his dad's credit card and running away to Europe. Always, there had been that escape hatch. They loved him, wanted the best for him, and would eventually forgive him and welcome him back. They had modeled God to him, but he had been too self-centered to realize it.

Here he was, on his own now, wondering when or if school would ever start up again. How would they notify the kids when it was time to come back? How many had disappeared? How many teachers? Would school ever seem normal again? And should he go to school? If Bruce was right and Nicolae Carpathia, who had just become the new secretary-general of the United Nations, could be the Antichrist, how long would it be before he signed some sort of an agreement with Israel?

If that came soon, there would be only seven more years of life on earth as they knew it. Did Judd need an education, or would he be wasting time in class while the world hurtled out of control? These were things he and the others were going to have to discuss with Bruce. But that would be later. Now it was time to get to Chicago and to watch the police sting LeRoy Banks and Cornelius Grey. It was a trap he had devised, which had impressed Sergeant Tom Fogarty.

Vicki had done a great job on the phone, pretending to be Maria Diablo, secretary to Tom Fogarty, "the attorney." Judd had thought of the fake name for her.

"Where did you come up with that name, anyway?" she said.

"*Diablo* means 'devil' in Spanish."

Vicki shot him a double take. "You think I'm a devil?"

"Hardly," Judd said, carefully picking his way through traffic. He wanted to look at Vicki, but there was still enough rubble and construction going on that he didn't dare take his eyes from the road.

Judd's grades had tumbled during the last year, but he had always been a good memorizer, probably from all the years he had spent in Bible memory clubs as a kid. That memory told him *diablo* was from the word *diabolical*, which meant "tricky" or "devious." That was what his plan was.

How many times had Judd's mother complained, "But you've got a good brain"? She used to say, "Use it like you used to, and your grades will shoot up."

He knew she was right, but because he had not been controlled by God back then, he had used the gift God had given him, that sharp mind, for his own purposes. He had devised a runaway plan, saved cash he got from the stolen credit card, and made his own plane reservations. Fittingly, God chose the middle of Judd's escape from his "awful" home life to send Christ and rapture the church.

If it hadn't been so devastating, Judd might have found humor in it. Though he knew the truth and what he had to do—receive Christ after all—still he found himself facing the despair of the loss of his family. Sometimes he caught himself in such a dark hole of sadness, despite finally settling things with God, that he wondered if he could go on.

Maybe, he thought, that was why God had, in essence, left him in charge of these other three kids. Without that responsibility, he wondered what would have become of him.

Keeping track of Ryan and Lionel alone kept his mind occupied much of the time. Then there was reading his Bible and studying what Bruce believed was crucial for him to know. Vicki didn't take any work. It was good to have someone close to his age to talk to, someone who seemed to understand him.

Judd pulled onto the expressway and found himself in that crazy traffic that had seemed to double since the Rapture. Where was everyone going? With so many having disappeared, it seemed strange that rush hour lasted all day and half the night now. People were desperate, frantic to see how this would all sort itself out. What would happen to their jobs, their companies, their careers, their plans?

It would be months, Judd figured, before the roadways were cleared of all the crashed cars and debris. It seemed all he and the others heard or saw on the news was crime and mayhem. Bad people took advantage of bad times, and times had never been as bad as this.

Judd was grateful Vicki was with him. On the one hand, he thought she was the type of girl he could get interested in, but on the other he realized that, had it not been for the crisis they found themselves in, they would never have even met. In fact, with him being from the ritzier part of Mount Prospect and her being from the trailer park, he wondered if they would have ever had anything to do with each other.

That all seemed so petty now. What was so important about how people looked and acted and dressed, or how much money their parents made, had nothing to do with their personal worth. Maybe some people would have been embarrassed to date someone from a lower class than themselves, but Judd had already seen how shallow that was.

When he talked to Vicki and spent time with her, he realized she was the same person whether she wore his mother's clothes or whether she wore her own. With or without makeup, with or without jewelry, who she was came through. At first her grammar was lazy and she used a lot of slang. But she knew better. It was clear she had a good mind. She had been even more rebellious than Judd, and it was clear she had seen how wrong she had been too.

Judd wanted to talk about the sting they were about to witness, but there was nothing to say. It had all been planned and laid out, and as far as they knew, neither LeRoy nor Cornelius suspected a thing. The only question was whether Talia had figured out what was happening. She had told Vicki that her brother and LeRoy were looking to cash in on insurance money. That had given him the idea of how to trap them. Would Talia catch on to that? And if she tipped the two guys off, would they avoid the sting or come in shooting?

For sure they would come armed. Both had enough enemies to make them look over their shoulders no matter where they went. That was why Sergeant Fogarty insisted that, while Judd and Vicki could come and watch, they had to be behind the protective one-way mirror, out of the way if anything bad happened.

Vicki wasn't sure yet what she thought of Judd. She had heard his story enough that she felt she knew it as well as her own. She was surprised at how similar they were, both having been rebellious kids. But she couldn't imagine why a rich kid would rebel against a setup like he had: his own room in a huge, expensive home, permission to drive his parents' cars, the latest clothes, the best gadgets, and never having to work. What was to rebel against? While she had always told herself she hated her parents' religion and rules, it was really where they lived that she hated.

Vicki never would have admitted that to a rich kid. In fact, she would have defended

the trailer park and its people over the pho-
nies who lived in the big houses and didn't
seem to care about anyone. Sure, her neigh-
bors could be loud and destructive, but look
what kind of lives they led. No one could get
ahead. They were all working to just get by.
Vicki had wanted to get out of that environ-
ment, and she had the sinking feeling it
would never happen.

Now, here she was, trying to convince herself she could fit into a different culture. But
was it just living in a rich kid's home that
made her look and think and act and even
talk differently? She knew better than that.
She had grown up overnight, and like Judd
often said, the things they used to think were
so important weren't so important after all.
Her biggest change, though she looked different, was inside. She didn't have to apologize
for being a trailer-park girl.

She certainly didn't feel as if she were
somehow from a lower class of people than
Judd was. He had treated her nicely from the
beginning, and she didn't get the impression
he was just condescending to her. He seemed
like a good kid, and he sure was smart. She
was too, if she could believe her teachers.
They had constantly told her she could do
better and that she wasn't working up to her
potential. But the idea of sitting up late at

night studying instead of running with her friends almost made her gag.

Now she felt like a fool. Like Judd, she missed the family she had squabbled with. She wished she had followed her teachers' advice. If she ever got the chance again, she would. Everything was different now. What a difference a few weeks made. More than that, she realized, the difference had come in an instant. Everything she ever thought or cared about changed when her perspective changed. And nothing could have changed her perspective more dramatically than millions of people—including her whole family—disappearing, just like they said they might someday.

Vicki shook her head as she thought about it. *When you're wrong, you're wrong,* she told herself.

"What?" Judd asked, startling her.

"What what?" she said.

"Out of the corner of my eye, I saw you shaking your head."

"I was just thinking," she said. "How different you and I are from who we thought we were not that long ago."

"I was just thinking the same thing."

"Are you scared?" Vicki asked, suddenly changing the subject.

"About this? Today, you mean?"

"Yeah."

"'Course. Aren't you?"

"Yeah," she said, "but it's kind of fun, and there's no way I'd miss it. It's like being in a TV show or a movie—only it's real."

Several minutes later Judd found the street he was looking for and parked three blocks away and around the corner. "We've got to hurry," he said. "Fogarty doesn't want us to be around here in case LeRoy or Cornelius comes early to check out the area."

TWO

In Place

LIONEL had the same fear Judd had, and at about the same time. As he sat at Judd's house with Ryan, waiting to hear how everything would turn out, he suddenly wondered whether Talia might figure this all out and spill the beans to her brother and LeRoy. She was not a dumb woman.

Lionel stood quickly. "I gotta get going," he said.

"What do you mean?" Ryan said. "You're not leaving me here alone."

"I have to, but just for a little while."

"No!"

"Yes! Now just wait here for me."

"Tell me what you're doing."

"If you have to know, I'm going to my house."

"What for? What if LeRoy and Cornelius are still there?"

"They won't be."

"You don't know that, Lionel. You're going to spook them!"

Lionel hesitated. "I think they'll be gone by now."

"You'd better check. Why not call them?"

Lionel thought a minute. "Good idea," he said. And he saw Ryan beam. Talia answered the phone. "Hey, Talia," he said.

"Lionel?"

"Yeah."

"What's up?"

"Thought I'd come and talk to you."

"Come on ahead. Nobody here but me."

"Really?"

Now Lionel didn't know what to do. He hadn't really wanted to talk to her. He had just wanted to distract her, to keep her from saying anything to LeRoy and Cornelius in case she had realized that they were being set up. It sounded as if she had never given that a thought.

"Yeah, come on over. I'm real sorry about André. You and your friends think LeRoy killed him."

"What do you think, Talia?"

"I don't want to think about it. I couldn't stand it if I thought LeRoy did something like that."

"You think LeRoy's never killed somebody before?"

"Not unless it was self-defense," she said. "Anyway, I was in love with André, and LeRoy knew that."

"Did André know it?"

"I hope so."

"I don't think he did," Lionel said. "You did a good job of hiding it."

Now she was crying. "Don't remind me," she said. "I was tryin' to control him, that's all. I figured if I made everything too easy for him, he would never do the right thing. André was a wild man, you know."

"I know."

"I wanted him to behave, to act right, to grow up, for me."

"He was tryin', I think. There at the end, I mean. Only somebody murdered him."

"Oh, no," she said. "He just died in that fire, that's all."

"Haven't you seen the news, Talia? He was found with a bullet hole in his neck, and he wound up bleeding to death. The fire would have killed him, but we pulled him out of there. We knew he was bleeding, but we didn't know why or where from. If we knew, we might have been able to stop the bleeding and save him."

"I'm sorry, Lionel."

"That LeRoy did this?"

"I'm not sayin' that."

"I am. How come you're alone there anyway?"

"LeRoy and Connie are in Chicago."

"What for?"

"I don't know. Some insurance thing. We're gonna be rich, so they tell me."

"I can't come over then, because I wouldn't want to be there when they get back."

"I think they're going to let you live here with us when they get a little money."

"And how are they getting this money?"

"Insurance, like I told you. It was Connie's apartment that burned, you know."

"How does that work? The insurance, I mean."

"I have no idea. All I know is that my brother was insured and he lost his apartment, so that's that."

"How much is it worth?"

"I don't know. Enough for them to risk going back into Chicago when lots of people, and the cops, are looking for them there."

"Why are the cops looking for them?"

"Lots of reasons. I wish they wouldn't go down there for a while, but when they smell money . . ."

"But you don't know how much?"

"All I know is that it's a lot, because they have to come there in person."

Lionel realized how strange this conversation was. Talia would be looking for some place to live tomorrow. Should he let her stay in his home, where she was now? No, that wouldn't be good. She had moved in with her brother and his friend, knowing they were up to no good, knowing it was wrong, and knowing it couldn't last. She would probably be arrested and held until the police determined whether she was in on any of the illegal stuff. Lionel didn't think she was.

"Well, I'll see you, Talia."

"You're not coming over?"

"Not tonight," he said. "Maybe I'll see you soon."

Lionel knew he would.

As soon as Judd and Vicki walked in the door of the storefront with "Thomas Fogarty, Attorney at Law" painted on the window, Tom Fogarty took them to the back, out of sight. He had the answering machine with him. "Here," he said to Vicki, pointing to a chair. "I need you to record a message."

As Fogarty was writing it out, Vicki asked what it was all about.

"It's important in a sting to play hard to get," the sergeant said. "If everything looks too easy for the mark—that's what we call the victim of the sting—he gets suspicious and might be scared off. We have to get these guys to come to us and keep after us until we arrest them."

Vicki recorded the script. "You have reached the law offices of Thomas Fogarty. We will be back in the office tomorrow. Please leave a message after the tone. Thank you."

"Won't this just make them mad and make them not show up?" she asked.

"The opposite. I'll be listening in. If they just seem mad and ready to hang up, I'll pick up and tell them I was just in for a second and heard their call. If they threaten to come and break in if no one's here, I'll let 'em. Once they get here, I'll pretend to be unable to find their file or their check, and you can bet I'll make them identify themselves thoroughly. They'll be working so hard to convince me they are who they say they are that they'll forget about any doubts they've had."

The other police officers came through the back, and Fogarty briefed everyone on where to be and what to do. Judd was so excited he could hardly stand it. The answering machine was hooked back up to the phone, and Fogarty turned around the Open/Closed sign in the window to indicate his office was closed. The phony secretary's desk was just messy enough to look real, and, of course, the chair was empty.

When everyone was in place, they waited.

"What makes you think they'll call?" Vicki asked.

"They're eager. They want to make sure we're here and that everything is ready for them. If they don't call, that's OK too."

But they did.

Sergeant Fogarty set the answering machine to pick up on the fourth ring, only prolonging their agony. As soon as the message started to play, Fogarty, the other cops, and Judd and Vicki heard LeRoy and Cornelius whining in the background.

LeRoy swore. "Oh, man, Connie! They can't be closed! What is this?"

At the tone, LeRoy yelled into the phone, "My name is Banks, and I had an appointment, so you better be in there when I get there!"

Judd was afraid Fogarty would be disappointed because he couldn't get on in time to tell LeRoy he would be there. But Fogarty apparently felt things were going perfectly.

"He said 'when I get there,'" Fogarty said. "They're still coming. He'll probably call one more time when they get close."

They waited several more minutes, and sure enough, the phone rang again. Same message. Same anger.

"If you ain't there when we get there, we gon' trash your office!" LeRoy shouted. "Now you should be expecting us! Don't make us break in there!"

Fogarty smiled.

Not long later, with everyone hidden, they heard the roadster slide up to the curb. LeRoy and Cornelius climbed out, looking enraged. They came up to the window and peered inside, and Judd heard LeRoy shouting and swearing all the way from inside. Cornelius had his hand in his belt, as if on a weapon.

LeRoy hurried to the car and popped the trunk, pulling out a long metal rod. He approached the storefront with it in two hands, like a baseball bat. With that, Tom Fogarty grabbed a file folder and walked out from the back room into the front office, not looking up, as if he was unaware anyone was even there.

LeRoy saw him and quickly held the rod out of sight behind his back. "Hey!" he hollered. "You open?"

Fogarty approached the locked door. "No! Sorry! Tomorrow!"

"I had an appointment!" LeRoy shouted.

"Today?"

"Yes! Today! Now let me in!"

Tom went to the secretary's desk and looked at the calendar, then slapped himself in the head, looking embarrassed and apologetic, and hurried to the door. Cornelius stepped in front of LeRoy as LeRoy skipped back to the car and tossed the metal rod in the backseat. "Now we're in business," Cornelius said.

Sergeant Fogarty had LeRoy and Cornelius right where he wanted them.

THREE

LeRoy Gets His

RYAN Daley was glad Lionel had decided not to go to his own home, where Talia Grey was alone. Ryan knew Lionel had intended to go without him, and Ryan had been left alone enough. It wasn't just that he was afraid, though that was a large part. But there was nothing to be afraid of at Judd's house. As far as he knew, none of the people who had invaded Lionel's house even knew about Judd or his place. Ryan felt safe enough there.

But also, Ryan had no brothers or sisters. He and his parents had been the extent of his family, and he'd had enough alone time when they were alive. That's why he had spent so much time with Raymie Steele, who had also disappeared in the vanishings.

Ryan was slowly adjusting to the fact that his parents were gone. They were still on his mind almost every minute of the day, and he often woke up between midnight and dawn, wishing this were all just a bad dream from which he would soon wake up. He had cried until he was sure there were no more tears, and then cried some more. He was embarrassed about that, being the youngest and noticing that the others didn't seem to cry much. But one night he had woken up with his sad thoughts and heard two of the others—he guessed Vicki and Lionel—sobbing in their beds too.

There was nothing wrong with that. What could be worse than losing your parents? Only missing out on going to heaven with them, Ryan figured. He put out of his mind the fact that his parents had not been Christians and that unless something very strange and very quick had happened before they died, it was likely they weren't in heaven now.

Ryan wandered into the kitchen, where he found Lionel eating a sandwich. "Want something?" Lionel asked, his mouth full.

"Nah. Just bored."

"Wish we were down there for the sting," Lionel said. "I want to see LeRoy get his."

Ryan nodded, and the phone rang. It was Talia. "For you," Ryan said. Lionel had given her his number the night she had driven him to see André.

Lionel pointed at the rest of his sandwich and nodded, and Ryan decided he was hungry after all. He finished the sandwich while Lionel talked with Talia.

Vicki Byrne had been involved in a lot of mischief in her young life, but she decided this was about as exciting and scary as anything she had ever done. She was crouched behind a low table next to Judd. They were in a perfect position to peek over the top and through a huge one-way mirror that gave them a view of the entire storefront and front door. They could hear perfectly because the whole meeting was being taped in that same room by the police. The storefront was full of hidden microphones so Sergeant Fogarty wouldn't have to wear a wire, as the police called it. In case the bad guys got suspicious and searched him, he would be clean.

Vicki watched as Fogarty unlocked the front door but opened it only a few inches.

"You can see there that we had an appointment," LeRoy said, attempting to come in.

"I'm sorry, gentlemen. It does say that on the calendar, if you are . . . ?"

"Banks. Banks and Grey."

"Yes, but Miss Diablo must have made a mistake. She knew I was off today."

"But you're here and we're here, so let's get this done."

"Well, I'd like to, but I have to be in court in half an hour and—"

"This ain't gonna take no half hour. We were told you had a check for us, and that's all we need."

"Really, gentlemen," Fogarty said, still standing inside the slightly opened door, "this would be much more convenient tomorrow or next week—"

"No!" LeRoy said. "Now we're here and you're here and we know you've got a check for us, so let's do this." He pushed his way past Fogarty, and he and Cornelius planted themselves in chairs at the side of the secretary's desk.

Fogarty was playing his part to the hilt. "To tell you the truth, gentlemen, I'm going to need you to refresh me on what this is all about."

LeRoy let his head roll back and he sighed as he stared at the ceiling. "Connie here, that's Cornelius Grey, he rents an apartment, well, he did anyway, on Halsted. It burned down."

"Oh yes, and this is about the insurance settlement then," Fogarty said.

"Exactly."

"And what is your stake in this, Mr., ah . . . ?"

"Banks. LeRoy Banks. I've been paying the rent for Mr. Grey here for several months, so—"

"And why was that?"

"What business is that of yours?"

"Oh, none, I guess. Proceed."

"Proceed? *You* proceed. Your secretary said she had a big check for us, so let's have it."

"Oh, I'm sorry, sir. Were you expecting the check itself today?"

"Of course! That's why we're here!"

"Well, this initial meeting was just for paperwork, signatures, identification, that type of a thing."

"So, we'll sign some papers. Let's get on with it."

"Well, the documents have to be forwarded to the home office for verification, and then the check can be released."

"So you're saying the check hasn't even been written yet? It's not here, like she said?"

"Oh, it's here, but if it's released before everything is verified by the home office, then I'm in trouble."

"You know what, Mr. Fogarty," LeRoy said, his face clouded with rage, "you're gonna be in trouble with somebody when we leave here, and you better hope it's the home office."

"But I can't—"

"Yes, you can. You give us that check based on our word that we are who we say we are, and you deal with the home office yourself."

"I'm afraid I can't—"

"You don't understand, Mr. Lawyer Man. We're not negotiatin'. We're walkin' out of here with the check."

Fogarty gulped and looked for the file. Vicki was impressed that there was an actual check in the folder. "OK," he said, "just let me see some ID so I'm covered."

Banks and Grey reached for their wallets and produced driver's licenses. Fogarty made a big show of meticulously copying down every detail. "Now, the check," LeRoy demanded.

"This is really highly irregular," Fogarty said.

LeRoy closed his eyes as if struggling for a last sliver of patience. "Just hand it over," he said.

Fogarty handed it to him, and LeRoy glanced at the figure. He smiled and showed it to Cornelius, then began folding it. Vicki

noticed three cops a few feet from her, guns
drawn, preparing to burst from the back
room. "Hey," Cornelius Grey said, "wait a
minute. What's that say?"

LeRoy had stood and was shoving the
folded check into his pocket when he pulled
it back out and studied it. Where his or
Grey's name was supposed to be were the
words *You're under arrest.*

"What?"

Fogarty flashed a badge from his pocket,
"LeRoy Banks, you're under arrest for the
murder of André Dupree and for arson in the
case of—"

LeRoy and Cornelius were reaching
for their weapons when the cops rushed
in. "Don't even think about it!" one shouted,
and the two were disarmed, handcuffed, and
led away. Vicki decided it was one of the
coolest things she had ever seen.

While Banks and Grey were being read
their rights, Vicki heard another police officer
on a walkie-talkie telling someone else to
"move on Talia Grey."

Lionel stood in the kitchen of Judd Thompson's house, watching Ryan finish the rest of

his sandwich. Lionel talked with Talia Grey on the phone, wondering what in the world she was so excited about.

"This is the weirdest thing," she said. "You have to see this. Maybe you've already seen it."

"What, what?"

"It's a videotape. Connie said it was in the VCR he ripped off from a house not too far from here. Guy on the tape says he's pastor of New Hope Church or somethin' and that if we're watchin' this, it's because he's gone. He's tellin' all the stuff we must be going through, and he's explainin' what happened, just like what my mamma used to tell me. This is so cool!"

"Yeah, I *have* seen it," Lionel said. "Like I told you before, I was the only person in my family who wasn't a believer. That's why I was left behind."

"Me too, I guess," Talia said sadly.

"You can do something about that, you know," Lionel said.

"Um-hm," she said, but from the background Lionel heard a doorbell and a loud knock. He recognized the doorbell as the one at his house, where Talia was. "Jes' a minute, Lionel," she said, and he heard rustling, as if she had slid the cellular telephone into a pocket. She had left it on.

As Lionel heard her walk through the house toward the door, he heard the shout, from a woman police officer. "Police, ma'am, open up!"

"I'm coming!" Talia managed. "Did something happen to—?" But her question was drowned out by louder banging on the door. "All right!" she said.

Lionel stood transfixed on the phone, listening as she opened the door.

"Talia Grey?" the policewoman asked.

"Yes! What—?"

"Miss Grey, you're under arrest for—"

"What? Under arrest? What'd I—?"

"For home invasion, burglary, accessory to murder. . . ."

"What? No! I don't know anything about—"

She grabbed her phone. "Lionel! Help! I'm being arrested."

Lionel wanted to tell her there was nothing he could do for her and that actually he was glad she was being dragged from his house. Maybe he could go home soon. But someone grabbed her phone and said, "Who's this?"

"Lionel Washington," he said. "You're at my house."

"Does Talia Grey have permission to be here?"

"No."

"And you're working with Fogarty?"

"Sort of."

"Thank you, son."

"Thank *you!*" Lionel said. And he decided life was crazy.

Judd was fascinated with how cops celebrated a sting that had worked well. They seemed unable to stop grinning. Fogarty and two others he had apparently known from his days in Homicide took Vicki and Judd to a coffee shop, where they sat reminiscing and congratulating each other. Everyone was impressed with the plan Judd had come up with, the performance by Vicki on the phone, and especially Fogarty's acting. "You sucked them right in," the older of his cohorts said. "You'll be back in Homicide in no time."

"That's what I want," Fogarty said. "But the way I hear it, most of you guys have been working double shifts, just like the rest of us working stiffs."

The cops sympathized with each other about how much work they'd all had to do since the vanishings. "What do you make of it?" Judd blurted, wondering if he should interrupt an adult conversation. But they had treated him almost like an equal up to now.

"Make of what?" Fogarty said, and Judd felt his face redden as everyone's eyes seemed focused on him.

"The disappearances. Where'd everybody go, I mean, in your opinion?"

Fogarty shook his head. "I've heard every opinion from space aliens to Jesus," he said. "One's as good as the other, I guess."

Judd was at a loss for words. What an opening! Bruce had told them to watch for opportunities to talk about the truth, and he predicted that at a time as dark and scary as this, there would be plenty of chances.

The younger detective said, "Seems like all we do is sit around asking each other if we lost anybody in the disappearances. Did you, by the way?"

"Me?" Fogarty said. "Yeah. Two elderly aunts. It was the strangest thing, something that would make you believe God *did* have something to do with this."

Something in the way he said that made the others laugh, and Judd wondered why. Was it a joke? Did Fogarty pray that he'd lose the two old aunts? He didn't get the humor.

"Why do you say that?" Judd asked.

"Oh, it's just that nobody in our family has ever been religious, except on holidays, you know. Going to church on Easter and Christmas was all part of the routine, but none of us claimed to be church people. But those two aunts of mine all of a sudden changed."

Judd thought the young cop looked particularly interested. Fogarty kept talking. "They started showing up to family reunions with their Bibles. That was kind of strange. We all had Bibles somewhere. The wife and I have one stashed in a drawer. It was a wedding gift, I think. That was weird, because this is a second marriage for each of us, and we didn't even get married in a church this time. But one of the aunts gave us that Bible. It was real pretty but it didn't look right sitting out, so we put it away."

Judd noticed the young cop lean forward, ignoring his dessert. He had blond hair and wore his side arm in a shoulder holster. "But what about these aunts?" he said. "What's their story?"

"Well, one of 'em had a husband die, and she kept living in their big old house for six or seven years. Then the other became a widow, and she didn't want to live in the same house she and her husband had lived in for so many years. So she moved in with the other. They were still young enough to be healthy, and they got out and about quite a bit. Somebody invited them to some kind of a religious meeting. It wasn't at a church. More like at an auditorium or something. Anyway, they started talking about getting saved and all that. They got religion, that's all I know. Started going to church and everything."

The young one, whom Judd thought he had heard Fogarty call Eddie, was still listening intently. Judd didn't want to admit he had forgotten the man's name already, so he asked if he had a card. The cop pulled one from his pocket. Judd studied it. His name was Archibald Edwards. No wonder he went by Eddie.

"But these aunts," Edwards pressed, "they disappeared, didn't they?"

"Yup."

"You ever consider maybe they *had* been saved? I mean, anybody else in your family vanish?"

Fogarty shook his head. "Well, my first wife. And I can't say I was sorry to see her go."

The others chuckled, all except Edwards. He was on the trail of something, Judd decided. "She was religious too, right?" Edwards asked.

Fogarty's body language made it appear he wanted to move on to something else, but he said, "Yeah, matter of fact she was. I think that's why we split. That and the job."

"Tell me about it," Eddie said. "This job's the enemy of marriage."

Fogarty nodded. "I was no saint. Gone all the time. I used to drink a good bit, you know."

The older homicide detective, a balding man with a huge belly, laughed. "That's an understatement," he said. "But it was what you did when you were drinkin' that cost you your first wife."

"All right," Fogarty said. "Enough said."

But Eddie the bloodhound was still on the scent. "So your wife and your two aunts—"

"My first wife."

"OK, your first wife and your two aunts are the only people in your whole family who were religious, and they're also the only ones who disappeared. Anybody else see a trend here?"

"We've heard and read all about the various theories," Fogarty said dismissively. "For all I know they were the only left-handers or redheads in the family too."

"Jeannie?" The old cop said. "Your Jeannie? She wasn't either one!"

"I'm just sayin'," Fogarty began.

"I'm telling you," Eddie said, "there were guys on the job who told me about God and everything, and those guys are gone. It's got me thinking."

"That's dangerous," the old cop said. Fogarty laughed.

"Yeah," Eddie said. "You guys laugh it off. What if it's true? What if this *was* something God pulled off? Where does that leave us?"

Judd turned to see if Fogarty had an answer for that one. Eddie must have taken Judd's look as agreement. "You brought this up, kid. What's your take on the vanishings? What do you make of it?"

FOUR

Meeting the Missus

HOMICIDE detective Archibald (Eddie) Edwards had posed the question. The ball was in Judd's court. Nervous and dry-mouthed as he was, he stepped and swung hard.

Judd told Sergeant Fogarty and the two detectives his whole story, from being raised in the church, to rebelling, to running away, to the Rapture, to getting home, connecting with Bruce Barnes, meeting the other kids, praying to receive Christ, and moving in together.

"So, you buy the whole package," Eddie summarized, reaching for his wallet and sliding his portion of the restaurant bill over to Fogarty.

Judd nodded, but it was the older detective

who spoke. "'Buy' is right. Man, have you been sold a bill of goods, kid."

In his peripheral vision, Judd noticed Fogarty nodding. Next to Judd on his other side, however, Vicki gently pressed her elbow against Judd's. He took that to mean she was with him, supported him, was glad he'd said what he said and that he shouldn't worry what anybody else thought.

Judd had hoped for more reaction than that from these guys. He didn't expect them all to fall to their knees or ask him to pray with them, but he wanted more than sarcasm or amusement. They were standing now and paying up. Tom Fogarty paid for Judd and Vicki. As they made their way out, Eddie got between Fogarty and Judd and put his arm around Judd. "You know what, Tom," he said, "this boy and his girlfriend and those other two kids ought to meet Josey."

The big detective, the older one, wheeled around and pointed in Fogarty's face. "Now, that's a good idea, Tom, and you know it. These kids ought to meet your wife."

"Excuse me," Vicki said, as quietly as Judd had ever heard her. He decided these guys must have intimidated her. "First of all, I'm not his girlfriend, and—"

"Ooh, ho!" the older detective said. "Touchy area, hm?"

"Second of all," Vicki continued, apparently unfazed, "why should we meet Sergeant Fogarty's wife? I mean, I'd like to and all that, but I was just wondering what made you think of that, Mr. Edwards."

"Call me Eddie. Well, first off, I know she'd love you and you'd love her. She's real warm and friendly. But ever since we've known her, she's been talking about stuff like this. We were surprised Tom even married her, she seemed so religious, and his first wife was way overboard. So, we figured—"

"And yet she disappeared, right?" Vicki said. "Along with Sergeant Fogarty's two aunts and the other people you used to work with who you thought were too religious."

"Yeah," Eddie said, pausing between the cars parked at the curb. "And I think there might be something to that. But Judd here himself said this pastor was left behind. And what about Josey Fogarty? She was all into angels and crystals and channeling and stuff."

"What they used to call New Age," Fogarty said. "Most of those people think the people who disappeared had bad vibes or something, so all the good people were left."

"We know from personal experience that ain't true," the big cop said, laughing loud.

Fogarty grinned and nodded. "Yeah. If

we're the good people, the world's in a sorry state."

"The world's in a sorry state anyway," Eddie said. "But I still think Josey and these kids ought to get together. I'm tellin' ya, you'd love her. But hasn't she been talking like this lately, Tom?"

Fogarty shrugged and looked away.

"C'mon, Tom," Eddie pressed. "You know it's true. Isn't she trying to drag you to some kind of a Bible study or something?"

"Better that than those channeling sessions she used to like," Big Man said, getting into his unmarked squad car.

Eddie got into the same car on the passenger's side, and Fogarty opened the door of his own squad car, prepared to take Judd and Vicki back to Judd's car. Judd suddenly felt overcome with an urge to not let Eddie get away without talking to him first. He asked Tom to wait a second and stepped to Eddie's window. "It was really great to meet you both," Judd said, reaching in and shaking both their hands. "Sometime I'd like to talk to you some more about those other cops who disappeared, Eddie."

Eddie met his gaze. "Yeah, let's do that. Seriously, I'd like that too."

Judd was certain that Eddie was curious and interested.

Lionel and Ryan sat watching television at Judd's house, waiting for news of the sting. More than an hour after it was supposed to have happened, they still had heard nothing. Lionel was worried. How long did it take to get to a phone and report in? He tried to make sense of what he was watching on TV, but it was all about the new head of the United Nations, Nicolae Carpathia. Bruce would have to explain this stuff to him. All Lionel knew was that since the Rapture there had been nothing on television except news, and he had never cared much for that before.

Finally, the phone rang, but it wasn't Judd. It was Talia Grey.

"Talia!" Lionel said. "I thought you got busted!"

"I did, fool. I get one phone call."

"And you call me? Shouldn't you call a lawyer?"

"A lawyer won't do me any good now, Lionel. I know we hardly know each other, but I got nobody else. My brother and LeRoy are in deep trouble, and LeRoy is going to think I set him up."

"Why?"

"He's always accusin' me of stuff like that. And Connie's no kind of brother. He'd just as soon get me in trouble with LeRoy than help me out."

"Well, I can't help you, Talia. I don't have money for bail or anything like that."

"I'm not worried about bail, Lionel. I'm better off in here than on the street, where LeRoy or Connie can have me killed."

"Your own brother wouldn't have you—"

"You don't know my brother. He's tried to kill me before. And he told LeRoy about my tryin' to signal you with your gym bag that one time."

"But they're both going to be in jail for years."

"I know. But they also know everybody on the street. They'll just have someone get rid of me, I know they will."

"What can I do?" Lionel said. "I can't let you stay in my house again if you get out. That's the first place someone would come looking."

"Don't you see, Lionel? I don't want to get out. I don't want to be anywhere where they can get to me. I don't care if I die in here. I might just kill myself."

"Don't be talking like that."

"I'm just sayin' I could die in here as easy as I could out there, and I know I'm not ready to die. You gotta help me get ready to die."

Lionel was speechless. She was flat out ask-

ing him to help her come to God. He had
never helped anyone do that before, and
while he thought he had an idea what to say,
he wasn't sure he could do it right then, right
there on the phone. He would need to be
sure he was doing it right, knew what to say,
what verses to use, and how to be certain
Talia understood and was being genuine.
"Where are you?" he asked finally.

She told him what precinct station-house
jail she was in.

"Can you have visitors?"

"Yes, come and see me."

"I'll try to get there tonight."

"Hurry."

"I will. I promise. Now can you tell me
something?"

"What?"

"Do you have any idea what happened
with your brother and LeRoy today?"

"All I know is what they told me here, that
they were busted in a sting operation and
they're at Cook County Jail."

"And everything went OK with the sting
and all that?"

"Well, it didn't go OK with Connie and
LeRoy, did it?"

"I mean, nobody was hurt or shot or anything."

"Not that I know of. Why? What'd you

hear? You hear somethin' different? How'd you know about this, anyway?"

Lionel guessed there would be no harm in telling her now. "Two of my friends were there. We helped set them up."

Someone said something to Talia about her time being up. "I gotta go, Lionel, but you have to tell me. Did they get the idea for this because I said LeRoy and Connie were tryin' to see about insurance money?"

Lionel's silence apparently told her what she needed to know. "Ooh," she whined, as she was hanging up. "I'm a dead woman."

"Still busy," Vicki said in Judd's car, after re-dialing Judd's home phone for the tenth time.

"Humph," Judd grunted. "You'd think they'd stay off the phone to wait for our call."

"We should have called them before we went out and celebrated with the cops," Vicki said. "Lionel probably got worried and is calling around to see if anyone knows what happened."

"Who would he call? He doesn't know any other cops that I know of. And Talia won't be reachable. Well, we'll be home soon enough. You know who you should call? Josey Fogarty."

"Why?"

"Invite them to my house."

"For when?"

"Tonight."

"Why not? You still have Fogarty's home number?"

Judd dug it from his wallet.

Lionel sat by the phone for five minutes after he had hung up from Talia. Finally he located Judd's car phone number and punched it in. Busy. He shook his head and called Bruce. He knew he wasn't supposed to tell anyone outside the case about what had happened, so he just asked for advice on what to say to Talia and how to say it.

"Mrs. Fogarty?" Vicki began. "You don't know me, but my name is Vicki Byrne and—"

"I know who you are, hon," came the friendly, husky voice. "I surely do. Tom just called to tell me everything went down fine and you kids were great. He thinks we ought to meet, you guys and me."

"We were thinking the same thing. How about tonight at Judd Thompson's house?"

"Tom's been there, right?"

"Right."

"I think tonight's wide open, Vicki."

When Vicki hung up she turned to Judd. "What a neat-sounding lady," she said.

When Judd got back into Mount Prospect, he went to the other end of town first and cruised slowly past Lionel's house. Two police paddy wagons were there, and a half-dozen or so uniformed cops were loading them with stuff from the house. Judd had no idea how they were going to tell what belonged to LeRoy's gang and what belonged to Lionel's family. Clearly, though, they were gathering evidence and trying to put the house back the way LeRoy and his cohorts had found it.

As Judd was finally pulling into his own driveway, the car phone rang. It was Lionel. "Where *are* you guys?" he demanded.

"Look out the window in the driveway," Judd said. "Be in in a minute."

When Judd traded stories with Lionel, he was as amazed as Lionel seemed. "So, you're going to see Talia at the jail tonight?"

Lionel nodded. "I'll see if Bruce can take me. He wants to meet with all of us sometime tomorrow, by the way. Big news. He said that guy my mom knew from the magazine, the one who called me once looking for her, has interviewed that United Nations guy."

"Carpathia? The one who was president of Romania?"

"Yeah, I think."

"What's the deal with him?"

"Bruce wants to tell us all together."

"What's the news guy's name?

"Cameron Williams," Lionel said.

"Really? That was the *Global Weekly* guy I saw on the plane. But he's not from here. I wonder how he knows Bruce. He must know Captain Steele."

Lionel shrugged. "So, anyway, I won't be here when the cop and his wife come. I'll have to meet her some other time."

Lionel overheard Judd call Bruce later and fill him in on everything that had happened that day. Bruce stopped by to pick up Lionel about half an hour before the Fogartys were to arrive and asked if he could talk to the four of them briefly.

Lionel followed him inside and was reminded why they liked Bruce so much. He was so earnest, so focused, and busy as he was, he seemed to care about everybody. Bruce gathered them in the living room. "We need to thank God for Judd's and Vicki's safety today, for Judd's chance to share his faith with the police officers, for Lionel's opportunity with Talia this evening, and for the rest of you with the couple coming over."

The five of them huddled, arms around each other's shoulders, as Bruce prayed. Lionel couldn't hold back the tears. This reminded him of Sunday nights with his family after a week of school and work and play and a whole day of church. His parents would bring everyone home and they would have some sort of a snack. It might be ice cream or popcorn or some special concoction his mother came up with. Then, before bed, they would gather, just like this. His dad or his mom, sometimes both, would pray for everybody in the family.

Even during the last few years, when Lionel kept to himself the terrible secret that he wasn't a believer, he had to admit he liked those family huddles. He wasn't rebelling against his parents, and he knew they cared for him. He had simply resisted God, and it had cost him everything. Thinking about that

warm, loving family he would not see until
he died or Christ set up his kingdom on
Earth made him weep now.

When Bruce finished praying, Lionel was
relieved to see that everyone else was emotional too. Even Bruce, who clapped him on
the back. "Let's go, Lionel," he said, and
Bruce led the way out of the house.

Vicki had a sudden thought as the kids were
doing a quick cleanup before their company
arrived. "Isn't this going to be, like, dinner-
time?" she asked Judd. "Do we have anything
planned?"

"Not unless they like TV dinners or fish
sticks or something," he said. "Maybe we
should order out for pizza or Chinese."

"Yeah," Ryan said. "Pizza!"

"That sounds kind of tacky," Vicki said.
"Oops, too late. They're pulling in."

Vicki was very nearly blown away by Josey
Fogarty. The woman appeared to be in her
late thirties, was of average height and trim.
She had pale blue eyes that reminded Vicki
of a summer sky, and she wore no makeup
or even lipstick. Her face was pale and cutely
freckled, her hair was a sandy blonde, and

there was plenty of it. She had a huge, easy smile that couldn't cover a certain sadness behind those eyes. But what got to Vicki most was Josey's forceful personality. She didn't hold back, but immediately took the initiative and took over, but in an appealing, inoffensive way.

"Why look at you all," she said, beaming. She took both of Judd's hands in hers and held them up to her cheeks. "You must be Judd, the great brain."

Vicki was amused at Judd's red face.

"And here's Vicki the redhead," she said, embracing Vicki. "Tom always calls you that as if it's one word.

"This must be Ryan!" She took his face in her hands and bent down so she could speak to him on his level. "You're only twelve? Why, you'll be tall as me inside a year!"

Vicki liked this woman already. "We, um, didn't really plan anything for dinner," Vicki said. "Did you already eat?"

"No," Tom said. "That's all right."

"No! It isn't!" Josey said. "We're starving and we're going to eat! What have you got around here?"

Vicki turned to Judd. He shrugged. "We could order out. . . ."

"No way!" Josey said. "Come on, now,

there must be something somewhere in this big ol' place. You got a freezer?"

"You mean a big one?"

"'Course! We don't want TV dinners and ice-cream sandwiches! C'mon, son, show me the big freezer. Where is it? In the garage? The basement? Where?"

It had been a while since Vicki had seen Judd flustered. "Well, ah," he said, "the big one's in the utility room downstairs."

"Well, la-di-da!" Josey Fogarty sang out. "This here house has its own utility room. I'm just in from outer space, Judd. Take me to your freezer!"

Vicki shook her head. Outer space was right. She was going to love this woman.

FIVE

New Truth

LIONEL liked having Bruce to himself for a while. If there was one thing frustrating about living with the three other kids, it was that he didn't get much time with Bruce, and when he did, it was usually shared with someone else.

Trouble was, Lionel couldn't think of much to say, now that they were on their way to Chicago to visit Talia in jail. All he did was fill Bruce in on the whole situation and tell him what Talia had said about her own spiritual life. "Her mother disappeared at the Rapture, and Talia says her mother tried to warn her. Now she thinks she has no chance because someone taught her that when Jesus raptured the church, the Holy Spirit was taken away."

"So she thinks no one can be saved now?"

Lionel nodded.

"We can counter that argument fairly easily, I think," Bruce said. And they lapsed into silence again.

Lionel wondered how Bruce found time do everything he had to do. But he was afraid to ask. Lionel figured the answer would have something to do with Bruce's not having a wife and kids anymore, and who would want to be reminded of that?

Bruce found a parking place several blocks from the precinct station house. "If there's any problem with your getting in to see her," Bruce said, "let me try a few angles."

Josey Fogarty had impressed Judd, too. From several items she had found in a freezer, Josey had cooked up some sort of a ground beef casserole with noodles and vegetables and cheese and all kinds of other good things that everyone seemed to enjoy.

Judd was also taken aback by Josey's beauty. He had never seen someone so pretty who was dressed and made-up so plainly (or, he should say, not made-up at all). Mostly, though, Judd simply loved being in her presence. She was warm and friendly, interested in everyone. If she made the others feel as warm and special as she made him feel, he assumed they all felt the same about her as he did.

"I'm here to see Talia Grey," Lionel said at the desk of the station house.

"She's not up for bail yet, son. Anyway, how old are you?"

"His age is not relevant," Bruce interrupted. "He's related to her former fiancé, who has died."

"I thought it was her former fiancé she was accused of murderin'," the desk sergeant said.

"She's not been accused of murder," Bruce said. "Now—"

"He'd have to be accompanied by an adult. Would that be you, Mr. Attorney?"

"I'm not an attorney. I'm clergy."

"Oh, why didn't you tell me, Father?"

"I'm not a pr—"

"Right this way. You weren't wearin' your collar, so I didn't even . . . I mean, you know. . . ."

The desk sergeant asked someone to cover for him while he led Lionel and Bruce into the bowels of the tiny jailhouse. "I don't know if you've been here before, Father, but we have only three men's cells and two women's."

"Thank you, Sergeant. So, is there a meeting room or . . . ?"

"Nothing sophisticated like Plexiglas walls or nothin', no. Just this little room over here, and we'll have a guy hanging around outside the door if you need anything. Now, I'm sorry but I have to pat you down for weapons and contraband. Rules, you know."

As helpless and panicky as Talia sounded on the phone, Lionel was surprised to see that she had slipped back into her more normal sassy and sarcastic tones. As she was led out of her cell by the matron and delivered to the desk sergeant, who walked her down the hall to the interview room, she said, "You all won't be seeing me much more in here, I'll tell you that right now! I got my people coming to get me out!"

The matron must have smiled or shook her head or something, because Talia immediately responded with, "Don't you be looking at me that way now! You just watch me! I'll be out of here soon!"

The desk sergeant told her to watch her mouth and manners and to behave herself in front of her company. Talia just cackled. "You don't have to be telling me what to do. Just mind your business."

Talia maintained her attitude until the
desk sergeant left and someone else was
assigned to stand in the hall. The door was
shut behind her, and she quickly sat down
and acted like a schoolgirl again. "I'm so glad
you came," she said. "I had no one else to
call. And this here, who's he?"

"This is my pastor, Bruce Barnes," Lionel
said. "I think you should talk to him about
your questions about heaven and all that."

"I already told you, Lionel, I don't have
any more questions about heaven."

"Why don't we sit down, Lionel?" Bruce
said.

Once they were seated, Talia started right
in again. "I'm going to need you to find me a
lawyer, preacher man," she said.

"I'll do what I can," Bruce said, "but
mostly I'm here to support Lionel and to
answer any questions you might have."

"And what makes Lionel think I have questions?" she said.

"You said you thought your mother was in
heaven," Lionel said. "But you were afraid
you had no more hope for some reason."

"I was always told that after the church got
raptured, the Holy Ghost would be gone. No
Holy Ghost, no salvation."

Bruce pulled a small New Testament from
his pocket and opened it on the table before

them. "Did you ever hear of a teaching from Revelation that says that during the time of the seven-year Tribulation God would raise up 144,000 witnesses who would go about the world evangelizing?"

"Yes," Talia said, "I think I did hear something about that somewhere along the line. Yes."

"Let me ask you something, Talia. What need would there be for evangelizing during the Tribulation if no one could come to Christ?"

Talia looked up and raised her eyebrows. "I never thought of that," she said. "How do these people get saved if the Holy Spirit is no longer here?"

"I'm not sure I agree that the Holy Spirit is gone," Bruce said. "I don't see that in Scripture, but even if it's true, apparently God finds another way to bring men and women to salvation, doesn't he? Otherwise, those 144,000 witnesses are out of business, aren't they?"

"I guess they are!" Talia said.

Bruce stood. "I'll tell you what, Talia," he said, "I know we don't have much time here, so I'm going to leave you and Lionel alone for a few minutes. Lionel, as you already know, is a new believer after growing up in a Christian home. It sounds to me like you are in a similar position to where he was not that long ago. It's important for Lionel to learn to tell others about his faith and how to come to Christ. I don't know how interested you are right now, but even if you are not, you would be doing Lionel a great service to simply listen to him and maybe even critique his approach. Perhaps you could help him learn to do this better. Could you do that for us?"

"Sure," Talia said.

Vicki was amused to see that even when they were finished with dinner at Judd's house, Josey Fogarty was still in charge. While her husband sat seeming bored or at least not surprised at her outgoing nature, Mrs. Fogarty began clearing the table and barking assignments. As usual, she was not in the least offensive. She had Ryan organizing the dishes, Vicki washing, and Judd drying, while she wiped everything down and even had her husband sweep the kitchen floor. "Make yourself useful, Tom," she said, smiling.

Vicki got the feeling that Josey was on a mission, had something to accomplish, something she wanted to do. That soon became clear. When the dishes were done and the place was spotless, she said, "So what do you want to do now, talk? That's what I want to do, talk. Where can we do that?"

"OK, Josey," Tom Fogarty said. "We can talk anywhere. Just slow up and sit down. We're not going anywhere until you get off your chest whatever it is you want to talk about."

For the first time, Josey looked slightly embarrassed. "Your friends thought I would enjoy talking to these kids, that's all," she said. "And I think I just might."

Vicki caught Ryan's eye and nodded toward a chair in the living room. Judd seemed to have already caught on that this woman was not going to be happy until she had nothing else to do but talk to everyone. Tom sat in an easy chair, Vicki in a wing chair, Judd and Ryan on the couch. Josey slid the footstool over from in front of her husband and sat on it, facing everyone.

"So you kids think the disappearances were what, something God did?"

Vicki blinked. Now there was an example of getting to the point! Vicki looked at Judd, who appeared at least temporarily speechless. He had been the one doing the talking to Sergeant Fogarty's coworkers after the sting. Vicki figured it was her turn now.

"That's exactly what we think," Vicki said.

"Everybody we know and loved who disappeared had told us about this and warned us. It happened just like they said it would, in a split second. They were gone, and we were left."

"But where are all the children?" Josey said. "The little ones, I mean. The babies, the toddlers, the . . . the . . ." She broke down and couldn't continue. She didn't hide her face or cover her eyes. She simply sat there open-faced, those beautiful blue eyes streaming.

Vicki glanced at Judd again, wishing Bruce was there. Judd appeared content to let Vicki have the floor. "We don't totally understand that either," she said. "Bruce Barnes, that's our pastor, says it has to do with something called the age of accountability. He says no one knows for sure about this, but it seems that God holds people accountable for what they know about him only if they're old enough to understand. We don't know how young a kid could be and still be held accountable, but, like you, we haven't seen too many kids left behind who are younger than Ryan."

Josey took a labored breath. "Did you know I lost two boys?"

Vicki shook her head. Why wouldn't Tom have said something?

"They were from my first marriage, and I didn't see them as much as I wanted to. I've always been curious about God, and I tried all kinds of religions and belief systems. Unfortunately, I was into some kind of strange stuff when my husband Steve left me for someone else. Even though he was living with another woman long before we were divorced, he got custody of Ben and Brad. I couldn't keep him from moving out of state, and I've been able to see the boys only about one weekend a month for more than two years."

"And your first husband?" Vicki said.

"What about him?"

"Was he left behind?"

Josey nodded. "Bless his heart, Steve blames himself. His young wife has already left him, so he has no one. But the boys, they were just gone from their beds the next day. He tried to file a missing person's report and was laughed off. Someone told him that if they filed missing person reports now, the cops would never get anything else done. Poor Steve had to swallow his pride and call Tom for advice. He wanted to know how he could get somebody somewhere to help him look for his kidnapped kids. Tom told him he'd maybe be a little more sympathetic if he didn't have a grieving mother to take care of too and if Steve would quit being so naïve as to think someone kidnapped millions of kids all at the same time."

"Basically," Tom interjected, "I just reminded him that he wasn't the only father to lose children that day. I mean, that may not have sounded too sensitive, but did he really think law enforcement was going to help him find his two kids when the whole world was grieving the loss of millions? Even Josey was realistic enough to know there was no future in driving six hundred miles to look for her boys."

"But don't think I didn't consider it," she said.

Vicki couldn't imagine the pain of losing your own child. It was hard enough for her to miss her big brother and little sister, and she felt guilty every day for the way she had treated her parents, right up until the time they disappeared. It was no wonder the world was in such chaos. There were millions of grieving mothers all over the world, hoping against hope that whatever these disappearances were, wherever their children had gone, it was not painful or frightening for them. The hardest part for parents whose children have been victims of crime, she knew from a mother in the trailer park, is imagining the fear and pain and loneliness of their last minutes alive. Vicki's neighbor, whose daughter had been kidnapped, said her worst nightmare was her complete inability to do anything for her child in the moment of her greatest need.

Vicki felt a flash of inspiration, a question crossing her mind that surprised even her. She hesitated, wondering if she should actually say it aloud. Before she could talk herself out of it, it talked itself out of her. "So, is that why you're so interested in knowing whether these people are in heaven? Because of your sons?"

"Of course," Josey said. "If I thought this was some kind of an alien invasion or attack from some foreign power, I'd rather die than think my boys are scared to death and suffering, or that they've been killed. They're dead to me unless they come back anyway, but I have to know they're all right."

"Nobody can tell you that for sure," Tom said.

"He's been saying that all along," Josey said, "and I know he means well. But someone must know. I'm not asking you to say something just to make me feel good, but—"

Vicki was glad when Judd finally decided to chime in. "If they disappeared right out of their pajamas in the middle of the night of the Rapture, then they're in heaven. You don't have to believe that, but that's the only explanation that makes sense to me."

"Well," Josey said, "thank you for that, anyway."

Lionel was talking straight with Talia Grey. He had run through all the verses Talia had heard in church from childhood. He started with the fact that "all have sinned and fall short of the glory of God" (Romans 3:23) and that "the wages of sin is death" (Romans 6:23). He said there is no other name under heaven by which we must be saved. He reminded her that she could not earn her salvation, that it is "not by works of righteousness which we have done, but according to His mercy" that God saves us. He added that Ephesians 2:8-9 makes it clear that we're saved by grace and that not of ourselves, not of works "lest anyone should boast."

With Bruce out in the hall, Lionel said, "You've got to be honest with me, Talia. I don't know what you and your brother and LeRoy were running out of my house, but if it was a burglary ring or dope selling or whatever, you're gonna wind up in jail for a long time, just like them. They're going to try to get you in on André's murder too, and—"

"There's no way! I loved him! I knew nothing about that! I would have tried to stop LeRoy if I'd known he was gonna do that."

"I'm saying that LeRoy and Cornelius will try to say you were in on it."

"How could they?"

"Criminals turn on each other all the time. André told me that."

"But Connie's my brother, and me and LeRoy go way back!"

"You know them better than I do. But didn't you tell me that Connie has already tried to kill you?"

Talia slapped a palm on the table, rousing the attention of the guard, who asked if everything was all right. "We're all right," Talia snapped. "Mind your business."

Lionel knew she was upset because she realized he was right. The only people she had left in the world would leave her high and dry if they thought it would do them any good. "Don't you think you ought to make sure about you and God before you go to trial or even to county jail? You never know what's going to happen to you."

"That's why I asked you to come here," she said. "I'll think about it."

"What's to think about? You grew up with this just like I did, and your mother was raptured just like she warned you about."

"I know."

"It takes more than knowing."

"I want to do this. But I'm not going to be pushed into it. I have to do this on my own."

"Fine. Then do it."

"Who do you think you are, talkin' to me like this? You're what, thirteen?"

"Talia, that has nothing to do with anything, and you know it. I'm being straight with you because you talk that way to people. I wish someone had talked to me this way before it was too late."

"Let me talk to the preacher man a second."

"Time's up," the guard said.

"No it ain't!" Talia exploded. "Not yet!"

"Yes, it is," the cop said, entering.

"I'm 'bout to get saved, so let that preacher in here now."

"You're what?"

"You heard me, now give me a minute."

The cop hesitated, looking at the glaring Talia and then at Lionel, who responded with a pleading look of his own.

"Awright, you trade places with the preacher man, and he's got two minutes."

SIX

New Lives

"HERE'S the thing," Josey was saying, crying openly. "I knew all that channeling, crystal, New Age stuff had nothing for me, but I was desperate. I had not been to church since I was a little girl, but I remembered there was supposed to be a God who loved me."

"Why didn't you go back to church?" Vicki asked.

"I believed what everyone else was saying. People said the church was full of hypocrites, that institutionalized religion caused more problems than it solved, that God was in all of us and that we could find him within ourselves. In fact, if some could be believed, we could be gods ourselves. It just seemed to me that the closer I got to finding the god within me, the farther I felt from a real God, if there was one. Then someone invited me to a Bible study. That wasn't scary. It didn't sound like church. It was just a place to read the Bible and talk about it."

"What have you learned so far?" Vicki asked.

"That's just it. I think I've got all the basics. If I can just accept the fact that there's nothing I can do to make this happen, I'll—"

"Make what happen?" Tom Fogarty said, suddenly interested. "What is it exactly that you want to happen, hon? You want to make sure there's pie in the sky by and by for you, or do you just want to cover all your bases so you'll get to see your boys again, in case they're in heaven?"

Josey turned to face him, and Vicki wondered if she was angry. She didn't appear to be, though she may have had a right to be. "No, Tom. I don't know. I want to be sure, and I want to know God. I have no idea where my boys are, but I have this feeling that if I can know God, I can know that too."

"I just worry," Tom said, "that this is simply another short-term interest of yours, something with an ulterior motive. Seeing your boys again is a worthy goal, of course, but you see what I'm saying."

"I'll tell you one thing, Tom," Josey said,

"this is no phase, no novelty. I'm desperate for God, and I won't stop searching till I find him. It's about the boys, yes, and it's about heaven, yes, and it's about fear over being left behind. But forgetting all that, I have to believe God knows me, knows about me, cares about me. If he loves me, I want to know it and know him."

Ryan surprised Vicki by talking directly to Tom. "What do you think, Sergeant Fogarty? Do you think we're all wrong about the disappearances?"

"I don't know what to think, Ryan. One of my detective partners, Eddie Edwards, I think he's really intrigued by all this. He thinks he has it figured out because so many people who talked about the Rapture were among those who disappeared. But there are also a lot of people missing who never talked about it. What about them?"

"You don't have to talk about it to believe it," Judd said. "My dad wasn't real big about telling other people, but he's gone."

"But if he knew, why didn't he say so? Why didn't people tell everyone about this before it was too late, if that is really what this was?"

"They're telling us now," Josey said.

Tom Fogarty's beeper sounded. "Excuse me," he said, glancing at it and then looking for a phone. He looked at Judd, who pointed to one on the wall in the kitchen. A minute later Tom came back with an apology. "I have to run," he said. "I can come back for you, Josey, or you can come along."

"I'll stay if you don't mind, hon," she said. "What's up?"

"Banks and Grey attempted a jailbreak while Eddie and two uniforms were escorting them to a deposition. Grey and Eddie were wounded. Grey's not serious. Eddie might be in trouble."

Vicki glanced at Judd, who had seemed so eager to talk to Eddie. Judd was pale, and he stood. "Can I come with you?" he asked.

"Sure."

Bruce was quiet on their way out of the jail. Lionel asked him what had happened with Talia, but he just put a finger to his lips. "Tell you in the car," he said.

After starting the car and putting on his seat belt, Bruce let his head fall back, and he sighed. He shook his head. Lionel waited, knowing Bruce would tell him when he was good and ready. "Well," Bruce said finally, "she prayed the prayer, as they say, and she said the right words, but I don't know."

"Don't know what?"

"Her motives or her sincerity. I think she's mostly scared of her brother and LeRoy. She might be scared of going to hell too, but there's nothing wrong with that. Who wouldn't be? Lots of people become believers based on that kind of fear. But I'm afraid what Talia really wants, why she wanted to pray with me instead of with you, is for me to get her a lawyer."

"Are you going to?"

"Oh, sure. I'll make a few calls. We have lawyers attending the church. But if she was sincere about her faith, I'd like to see her get serious about Bible study, get a chaplain to counsel her, get into a church even in jail. I assume she's not into this crime spree and the murders as deeply as her brother and LeRoy are—at least I hope she's not—but still she could be in jail a long time. She'd better not wait till she's free to start exercising her faith. You remember the parable of the seed that falls on the different kinds of soil? I can't think of anything or any place worse for new seed than prison. She could come out of there hard as a rock, where the seed can't grab hold and sprout."

Judd noticed that Tom Fogarty's own car was the same size as his squad car but a lot roomier. There was no radio, no shotgun, no computer screen, none of the stuff that crowds the dashboard of a police cruiser. Tom looked worried and drove fast. Judd was buckled in, but he also braced himself and tried to engage Tom in conversation.

"What'd they tell you about Eddie? How bad is it?"

"Not good," he said. "You know officers don't carry weapons inside the jail, because if a prisoner jumps you and disarms you, you've got trouble. So Eddie and whoever else he was with would have checked their guns with the jailer, then escorted the hand-cuffed prisoners down the hall and into the parking garage for a ride to the courthouse or wherever they had to go."

"So where would Grey and Banks have gotten guns?"

"Probably from a cop either in the garage, the elevator, or even one of the vehicles."

"Those jailbreaks never work, do they?"

"Not usually. A guy jumped a woman officer in the elevator downtown once and disarmed her, killed her, killed a guard, and wasn't shot himself until he had gotten free and was out on the ramp. I hope he enjoyed his freedom. It lasted maybe fifteen to twenty seconds."

"What kind of a shoot-out was this one with Grey and Banks?"

"Quick, I guess. They usually are, but sometimes they get to be drawn-out things. They tell me one of them, probably Banks, grabbed someone's gun and shot Eddie in the face before he had a chance to respond. Three cops fired at the prisoners, apparently blowing off Grey's ear. Banks immediately surrendered."

"Sounds like the whole thing took just seconds."

"Probably, but depending on where Eddie was hit, it could last him a lifetime."

"You don't know how serious it was?"

"He's unconscious, that's all I know. And that's not a good sign. Sometimes these facial wounds are bloody but don't do much structural or organ damage unless they lodge in the eye or the nasal passage. If he's unconscious because of the wound, it could be brain penetration. That would be bad. He might never regain consciousness."

"Could he die?"

"I don't even want to think about that. He's the youngest guy in Homicide, but I worked with him for years. Met him when he first came over. Energetic, smart, good team guy. A cop's cop. You know what the worse thing is? I got a call earlier today from downtown, congratulating me on the Banks bust. Said I was next in line to get back into Homicide but that they didn't have a spot for me just yet. They said to be patient and I'd get my chance again."

"And you wanted that?"

"More than anything, but I sure don't want it this way."

It took Tom just minutes to get onto the expressway, and he wasn't afraid to take chances, to ride on the shoulder even without an emergency light. If he got stopped, Judd assumed, he would just let the officer know he was on the job, and he would be waved on.

Judd wanted to find out why Fogarty seemed so uninterested in God when his wife seemed so eager to learn everything she could. But Judd didn't know how to ask. "You know, Mr. Edwards seemed really interested in talking with me about the Rapture and stuff."

"I noticed that."

"Was he just being polite, teasing me?"

"I don't think so. He's not that kind of a guy."

"But even though your wife is interested, you don't seem to be."

"I'm not."

Well, Judd thought, at least that was honest. Tom was a straightforward kind of a guy. He liked directness and wasn't afraid of disagreement. "Why not?" Judd asked.

"You really want to know?" Fogarty asked.

"Yeah, I do."

"It might offend you. I can see you're really into this. I wouldn't want to be the one responsible for changing your mind."

"You couldn't."

"Fair enough," Fogarty said. "I'll tell you exactly why. I was raised in a church where I was taught that God was love, but also that if you died with one sin on your soul, you went to hell. I couldn't make that compute. I quit the church as soon as I was old enough to make my own decisions. I still carried around in my head the belief that there was a God, but that he was a God of love. Not an angry judge, not a crabby parent. Not someone who would create a person and burn him up later."

Judd wanted to argue. Bruce had taught the kids that hell was a judgment for sin and that it had to do with justice. But God didn't want anyone to die and go to hell. He had given the world so many chances to be saved that there was no reason anybody had to go to hell. Judd sat silent, but Fogarty had just warmed up. As he wheeled around traffic and went as fast as the jam would allow him, he continued.

"I was OK with that view of God for a lot of years, even after I became a cop. But then stuff started to not add up. When I got into Homicide I saw stuff nobody should ever have to see."

"But you like it. You want to get back into it."

"It's where the action is, and I'm good at it. I feel I'm accomplishing something and help-ing people when I solve a case and put bad guys away. But I sure grew up in Homicide. I quit thinking of God as someone who made sense. In fact, I don't know if I believe there's a God at all anymore. How could there be a God, in charge of everything, who would allow the things I've seen? People blud-geoned and mutilated, usually by someone they love and trust. I've seen parents murder their own children, children murder their own parents. I've seen people go through things that no one should ever have to endure. Where is God in that?"

Judd had had the same questions, and he wasn't sure of all the answers. But he knew what Bruce would say. He didn't know the

exact words and didn't know if he could back
up those words anyway without being a
Bible student like Bruce. But he had learned
that just because God allowed something
didn't mean he was for it. God truly was a
God of love, and seeing people murder each
other had to make him sad. But he had temporarily given control of the world to Satan.
God would win in the end, but in the meantime, things were going to get only worse.

Judd knew if he said that, he would sound
like some idealistic young kid who believed
everything he heard. He had not seen the
things Tom Fogarty had seen. He didn't
know what he would think if he did see
them.

"I'm glad for you that you have something
you believe in," Fogarty said. "If it works for
you, fine. If it works for Josey, I'll be thrilled.
Nobody that wonderful should have to go
through what she's going through. It's been a
long time since I've seen her come to life the
way she did around you kids today. She
rarely smiles anymore, but the way you saw
her today, that's the way she used to be all
the time. But parents are not supposed to
outlive their kids. It's too much to ask of a
mother to have her children disappear. And
it's happened all over the world. And you

want to tell me the loving God of the universe did this on purpose? For what?"

"To convince you once and for all," Judd said.

"Convince me of what?"

"That he's real. That he was willing to give up his Son and that he will give you chance after chance to believe that he is who he says he is. He said he would rapture his church, and he did. He's going to come back again in seven years or so, and that will be the last chance of all for anyone who will still be alive."

"Good. I'll wait until I'm convinced."

"But very few people are going to still be alive by then. Bruce Barnes thinks only a quarter of the world's population will still be alive when Jesus gets here."

"This is your loving God doing this? Wiping out three-fourths of the world after already taking away the believers? I don't get it."

"He's not doing it. He's allowing it to get our attention."

"Call it whatever you want. It sounds crazy to me."

Judd was frustrated. He knew he wasn't explaining it well. On the other hand, Bruce had told him and the others that it wasn't up to them to convince people. They were just supposed to lovingly tell them the truth. Changing people's minds and hearts and getting them to come to Christ was God's work. We do our part and God does the rest. It seemed to Judd that neither he nor God was getting through to Tom Fogarty.

A few minutes later they pulled into the front circle of a huge hospital in the Loop. A uniformed cop hurried over to tell them to move the car, but he backed off when he saw Fogarty's badge. "Here to see Eddie?" the cop said. "He's out of Emergency, but he's in Intensive Care. Fourth floor, south wing."

As Judd and Fogarty hurried to the elevator, Fogarty said, "Unfortunately, I know exactly where ICU is. Been there many times."

Desk personnel tried to stop them in the lobby, but again, Fogarty just flashed his badge and kept moving. When the elevator doors opened on the fourth floor, Judd followed Tom down the hall past dozens of uniformed cops lined up on either side of the corridor. "Everybody on the clock?" Tom said, kidding them. "Nobody out serving and protecting while they're making their money?"

"We're standing behind your buddy, Tommy. Show a little respect."

"How's he doin'?" Fogarty asked, not slowing to listen.

"Not so good," another said. "If he don't make it, I know two bad guys who are never gonna get out of the can alive."

"Now you know better than that," Fogarty said. "I'd be right in there with ya if that was the answer, but you know Eddie wouldn't want that."

"Just the same . . . ," someone grumbled, leaving the end of the thought unspoken.

They reached the door of the ICU room with "Edwards, Archibald" on the nameplate.

"What's happening?" Fogarty asked the cop at the door.

"They're telling us nothing. He's still unconscious. No promises."

"Where'd he take the bullet?"

"Through the cheekbone."

"Ouch. Brain damage?"

"They're not saying, but what else can it be, Tommy? Point-blank range."

Fogarty swore, then glanced at Judd and apologized.

"Excuse me, gentlemen," a doctor said, trailed by a nurse and what looked like an intern, a young woman. He pushed his way through, and the three slipped inside the door.

Before the big door swung shut, Judd

peeked in and saw a male nurse on a stool, studying a printout as it came from a machine near the bed. Judd would not have recognized Eddie. He lay still, on his back, hands at his sides, tubes running to both arms, oxygen mask in place. His chest did not seem to be moving. His eyes were closed. No movement. Worse, just before the door eclipsed the view, Judd saw the nurse look directly into the doctor's eyes and shake his head.

Vicki wished Bruce and Lionel would get back soon. Besides wanting to know what went on with Talia Grey, she wanted help with this lovely troubled woman. Josey Fogarty sat there with Vicki and Ryan, pouring her heart out and virtually pleading with them to lead her to Christ. Vicki decided she could not and should not wait any longer. Using the same verses Bruce had taught Lionel, and starting with the basics, she asked Josey if she saw herself as a sinner in need of someone to forgive her and save her.

"I surely do," Josey said. "I surely do."

SEVEN

The Good News and the Bad News

VICKI had listened intently during Bruce's training sessions with his new young charges, and she had wondered if she was up to a task like this. She was not prepared to lead someone to Christ just yet, though she agreed with Bruce that there could be no higher privilege for a Christian.

She was brand-new in the faith, and she had already been grounded in the basics, but she really hoped Bruce would arrive soon and take over with Josey Fogarty. Silently, Vicki prayed earnestly. Her major request was that Bruce bail her out. But short of that, she pleaded with God to remind her of the verses, to give her the words to say, to assure that she would say whatever she was supposed to say and avoid whatever she was not supposed to say. The last thing she wanted was to somehow mislead this precious woman who so desperately wanted to come to God. Vicki didn't know what all that New Age stuff was that Josey had talked about, but she sure knew it was not part of the true gospel as she knew it.

Vicki didn't want to stall any longer when it was obvious how ready Josey was. So once she had established that Josey knew her position before God and how it could change, she plunged ahead. When she was finished explaining how to pray and receive Christ and Josey bowed her head and closed her eyes, Vicki glanced at Ryan. She was encouraged to see a look on his face of wonder, of emotion, of encouragement to her. It was as if he told her with his eyes that he felt privileged to be there.

Vicki asked Josey if she wanted her to lead her in the prayer of acceptance of Christ, and Josey surprised her. "You know, hon, I don't think so. I think this is somethin' I got to do for myself. If God loves me and cares about me personally, like you say, I want to talk to him myself. So I think I'll just start in."

Vicki lowered her head and listened.

"God," Josey whispered, her voice thick with emotion, "you know I've been looking for you for years, and I'm glad to hear you've been looking for me too. I know I'm sup-

posed to start by telling you I know I'm a sinner and that I need you. Part of me always
wanted to do good and be known as a nice
person, but I knew myself then and I know
myself now. I've never been able to be the
kind of person I know you would want me to
be. Thank you for dying for my sins and for
forgiving me. Forgive me for not being ready
when you came for your people. If you will
accept me, and I believe that you will, I offer
you the rest of my life."

Vicki wept as she heard Josey go on to pray
for Steve and Tom. And for her sons. She
prayed for Eddie. She prayed for "these three
kids I've just met and for the one I haven't
met. And for their pastor."

Vicki thought it the most impressive prayer
she'd ever heard, especially coming from
someone who was taking her first step as a
believer. Josey ended by saying, "I don't even
know how to sign off, so I'll just say good-
bye and I'll be talking to you again soon.
Amen."

Vicki looked up through her tears as Josey
sat there, her cheeks wet too. "Was that all
right?" she asked, timidly.

"That was perfect," Vicki said, and they
hugged each other. Ryan looked on, appearing to be fighting tears too.

"C'mere, Ryan!" Josey said, opening her

arms wide. He rushed to her, and the three of them embraced.

Judd wondered how long Tom Fogarty would wait for the doctor to emerge from Eddie Edwards's hospital room. He was worried Tom would just barge in. Instead Tom approached the nurses' station around the corner. "Is there some reason we're getting no hard information from the doctors about Detective Edwards?" he asked.

The woman in charge looked sternly at him. "And you are . . . ?"

Tom showed her his badge and told her. She glanced down the hall and removed a chart from a rack. She motioned him closer with a nod and glared at Judd as he also approached, but Tom said, "He's with me."

She flipped open the chart. "We're talking about Edwards, Archibald, are we not?" she whispered.

Tom nodded.

"We are off the record, sir, and nothing you hear from me should be considered official or final or quotable. Is that understood?" Tom saluted her. "You're not related, are you?"

"No, why?"

"Because a next of kin would not want to hear this. I'm not a doctor, you understand, but I've been an R.N. for thirty-five years and I can read a chart. This man is not going to regain consciousness, and that's the kindest thing God can do for him at this point, short of just taking him."

"Ma'am?"

"You sounded like you wanted the truth, young man. I'm giving it to you. This patient took—" she began reading—"'a high-speed, hollow-point, nine-millimeter shell to the cheekbone from less than six feet away, fired from a Beretta service revolver.'"

"A Beretta is not a revolver," Fogarty said, "but otherwise I'm following you."

"I'm just tellin' you what it says. I'm no firearms expert. What I understand is that this bullet is made that way for maximum speed and shattering ability upon impact."

Tom nodded, looking glum.

She read again. "'The bullet entered at an acute, nearly vertical angle, passing just under the right cheekbone and bursting into fragments that destroyed the olfactory canal, the entire right eye socket, and extending into the frontal lobe of the brain before exiting through the top of the skull.'"

She let her reading glasses slip off and dangle at the end of the strap around her neck. "Need I be more specific?"

Fogarty shook his head. "It'll be more merciful, as you say, if he passes. Am I right?"

"I'm afraid so, son. I'm sorry."

Tom thanked her and turned away, and Judd noticed he walked stiffly, as if he had to plot each step. "You want something to pray about, Holy Joe?" he said. "You pray Eddie Edwards dies before his family has to see him like that."

Judd didn't want to pray for that at all. He wanted a miracle. He wanted that man who had just hours before seemed so interested in the things of God to regain consciousness, to know how close he came to death, to be spurred to take action now and receive Christ.

As he and Fogarty went back around the corner, the doctors and the nurse emerged from Edwards's room. They were met by the same heavyset detective who had been in on the sting that day and had been with them in the diner. "There's Willis," Fogarty said. He looked grave.

"I'm the ranking officer here," Willis told the doctor. "And I want to tell these cops something concrete."

"Is there a next of kin?" the doctor said quietly.

"Oh, no," Willis said.

"Come on, sir, we've all been through this before. I can't be making statements the next of kin have not heard."

"Tell me and I will tell the next of kin."

The doctor pulled a notepad from his pocket. He spoke so softly that only Willis, Fogarty, and Judd could have heard him. "Time of death, 8:55 p.m."

The doctor moved away, and the sea of cops surged toward Detective Willis. "You people are to be back on the street immediately. We will broadcast an update in fifteen minutes. Be somewhere where you can hear it."

"Is he dead?" someone called out.

"Don't start acting like the press," Willis growled. "Now get going!"

Lionel and Bruce were near Judd's home when the report came over the radio about the jailbreak attempt a few hours before. "An update on that story," the newsman said, "is that the police officer wounded in the brief shoot-out fights for his life at this hour."

Lionel and Bruce looked at each other. "Unbelievable," Bruce muttered. He asked

Lionel to call Judd's house and tell them to turn on the news.

"Lionel!" Ryan said, blurting all the news at once. "Judd and Tom went to see the cop shot in the escape thing, and Tom's wife is here and she just prayed to accept Jesus, and—"

"We're on our way, Ryan," Lionel said.

Judd sat stunned in the quiet car as Tom drove him back from Chicago. Judd was frustrated that he had not been able to talk to Eddie about God when he had seemed so interested. How many other ways did God have to use to show him that no one was guaranteed any time anymore? They had driven almost an hour before Tom spoke.

"Explain that one to me," he said, "if you know the mind of God so well."

"I never claimed that, Mr. Fogarty, but it's sure a lesson, isn't it?"

"Yeah? What's the moral of this story?"

"Don't wait. If you're curious about God, don't put off finding out about him."

"So a great young cop dies to warn me to find God? I don't think so."

Judd knew Fogarty was in too much pain

to be reasoned with just then, so he fell silent. Tom turned on the radio when they reached the suburbs and soon heard the news they had known before anyone else. When they pulled into the driveway at Judd's, Bruce's car was in the driveway. "I want you to meet this guy," Judd said, assuming Tom would at least come in to get his wife.

"I really don't feel like seeing anyone right now," Tom said. "Would you mind just sending Josey out?"

Judd hesitated, then said, "Sure."

As he was getting out of the car, Tom called out to him. "Judd, I'm sorry if I took this out on you a little. I don't want you to lose your faith or anything."

Judd didn't know what to say, so he just nodded and ran into the house. There he found everyone beaming and was quickly filled in on what had happened to Josey. She was sitting with an arm around Lionel, whom she had finally met and who was looking pleased but uncomfortable with her attention.

"I hate to be the one with the bad news, Mrs. Fogarty and everyone," Judd said, "but your husband's waiting for you in the car, and he's pretty upset over Eddie's death."

Josey's smile faded as fast as it had come.

"Oh, no," she said, over and over. And she hurried toward the door.

"Take a minute and let us pray for you," Bruce said, and he and the kids huddled again, this time with her in the middle of them, and prayed for her in her new faith. Bruce prayed for her husband and for the Edwards family.

A minute later Josey was gone, and Judd and his friends sat with Bruce, exhausted and silent. "I've got to get going," Bruce said finally. "Big day tomorrow. And then the next night we're meeting, just the five of us. I have so many things to tell you. Huge news about the Antichrist and the Tribulation and other things in prophecy. You learned today that not everything in the Christian life is neat and tidy. Things happen that we don't understand, we don't like, and we can't explain. God's ways are not our ways, and his thoughts are not our thoughts.

"Not that long ago I never knew anyone who had been the victim of a violent crime. I never knew anyone who had been killed, murdered, or even threatened. Now Ryan has had his parents both die, Lionel has lost an uncle to murder, and Judd has lost a new acquaintance. It's as if God is using this period in history as a crash course in life and death. We tell people they don't have a lot of time to be deciding what they will do about Jesus, and then it is proven to us every day."

Judd collapsed into bed that night with mixed emotions. He missed his family, but he was grateful for his new friends, for Bruce, and for his own assurance of heaven. He wished he knew the mind of God better and could understand why things happened the way they did—either that or to be able to somehow explain them to people like Tom Fogarty.

Judd was fascinated by prophecy and the fact that he and his friends were living right in the middle of it every day. He knew Bruce's teaching on the Antichrist would be troubling and scary, but he would sure rather know than not know what was coming.

EIGHT

Revealing the Enemy

THE following Sunday, Judd had the idea
Bruce was holding back with the congrega-
tion that packed the pews at New Hope Village Church. Oh, Bruce was as earnest as
ever. But he had told Judd and the other kids
that he suspected Nicolae Carpathia, the new
head of the United Nations, was the Antichrist. Bruce swore them to secrecy and said
the only others who knew how he felt were
four adults who formed a sort of inner circle
within the church.

When Judd heard Bruce's message that
Sunday, he realized the point of all the
secrecy. Bruce outlined from Scripture what
he believed were the characteristics of the
Antichrist, and anybody with a brain could
see he was talking about Carpathia. But
Bruce was careful not to use his name or the

name of the organization he ran. Judd decided that Bruce had big plans and that he wanted to survive in order to carry them out. He wanted to expand his ministry, to branch out and teach small groups in homes all over America and maybe the rest of the world. If he said from the pulpit of a big church exactly who he thought was the Antichrist— and if he were right—his life would be worthless.

Bruce had promised the kids that he would show them tapes from the big news shows, tapes he had been gathering for days. Somewhere in the middle of all his study and ministry, Bruce had found the time to edit and put the tapes in order. He told Judd that with just a little of his own explaining, he believed Judd and the other three would know for sure what to make of Carpathia.

Monday afternoon the kids met with Bruce, and only Bruce. At other times there were a few other adults or Bruce's secretary in with them. But not this time. Bruce had rigged up a TV set and a VCR, and he sat with a pile of notes on a yellow legal pad, and of course his Bible.

After they brought each other up-to-date on their lives, their study, and their prayer requests, they prayed. Then Bruce began with a tape from *Nightline* the night after Carpathia appeared at the United Nations. "It shows this guy as a master communicator. I know you all saw his address to the United Nations. Remember, he was just a guest. That speech and the way he carried himself made them beg him to take over. Watch now, and see how well coached he is. Either that, or he's a natural, born for television."

Carpathia looked directly into the camera whenever possible and seemed to be looking right at the viewer. Judd couldn't take his eyes from the handsome, engaging, often smiling face. He found himself wishing such a nice, well-spoken, and seemingly kind man didn't have to be a bad guy. And he even found himself wondering if Bruce could be wrong. He hoped so, but Bruce hadn't been wrong about much so far.

The interviewer was a newsman named Wallace Theodore. He began, "Your speech at the United Nations, which was sandwiched between two press conferences today, seems to have electrified New York, and because so much of it has been aired on both early-evening and late-night local newscasts, you've become a popular man in this country seemingly all at once."

Carpathia smiled. "Like anyone from Europe, particularly Eastern Europe, I am amazed at your technology. I—"

"But isn't it true, sir, that your roots are actually in Western Europe? Though you were born in Romania, are you not by heritage actually Italian?"

Bruce pointed the remote control at the TV and paused the tape. "Remember what I taught you about the Antichrist?" he said. "That he would have Roman blood?"

The kids nodded, and Bruce turned the tape back on.

"That is true," Carpathia was saying, "as is true of many native Romanians. Thus the name of our country. But as I was saying about your technology. It is amazing, but I confess I did not come to your country to become or to be made into a celebrity. I have a goal, a mission, a message, and it has nothing to do with my popularity or my personal—"

Bruce fast-forwarded the tape, explaining that Carpathia was defending his submitting to an interview with *People* magazine. Bruce started the tape again as Carpathia was saying, "I am on a crusade to see the peoples of the world come together. I do not seek a position of power or authority. I simply ask to be heard. I hope my message comes through in the article in the magazine as well."

Vicki interrupted by raising her hand.

"Now, see?" she said. "What's so wrong with that? Isn't that what we want to hear someone say at a time like this?"

"Sure," Bruce said, "but keep listening carefully."

Mr. Theodore said, "You already have a position of both power and authority, Mr. Carpathia."

"Well, our little country asked me to serve, and I was willing."

"How do you respond to those who say you skirted protocol and that your elevation to the presidency in Romania was partially effected by strong-arm tactics?"

"Whoa!" Lionel blurted, shaking his head. "Pause that. He totally lost me. What is he asking?"

Bruce chuckled. "Let me interpret. Protocol is the standard and accepted way of doing things. Romania had a democratic election, but some people say that Carpathia somehow got around that by getting himself put in as president, even though it was in the middle of another man's term in office. Carpathia was just a member of the lower house of government there before that."

Lionel nodded and the tape began again.

Carpathia responded, "I would say that that is the perfect way to attack a pacifist, one who is committed to disarmament not only in Romania and the rest of Europe but also globally."

"In other words," Bruce interjected quickly, "he says he doesn't believe in war and weaponry."

"So you deny," the newsman came back, "having a business rival murdered seven years ago and using intimidation and powerful friends in America to usurp the president's authority in Romania?"

"The so-called murdered rival was one of my dearest friends, and I mourn him bitterly to this day. The few American friends I have may be influential here, but they could not have any bearing on Romanian politics. You must know that our former president asked me to replace him for personal reasons."

"But that completely ignores your constitution's procedure for succession to power."

"How they elect a president," Bruce explained.

"That was voted upon by the people and by the government and ratified with a huge majority," Carpathia said.

"After the fact."

"In a way, yes. But in another way, had they not ratified it, both popularly and within the houses of government, I would have been the briefest reigning president in our nation's history."

Theodore asked him, "Why the United Nations? Some say you would have more impact and get more mileage out of an appearance before our Senate and House of Representatives."

"I would not even dream of such a privilege," Carpathia said. "But, you see, I was not looking for mileage. The U.N. was envisioned originally as a peacekeeping effort. It must return to that role."

"You hinted today, and I hear it in your voice even now, that you have a specific plan for the U.N. that would make it better and which would be of some help during this unusually horrific season in history."

"I do. I do not feel it was my place to suggest such changes when I was a guest; however, I have no hesitation in this context. I am a proponent of disarmament. That is no secret. While I am impressed with the wide-ranging capabilities, plans, and programs of the United Nations, I do believe, with a few minor adjustments and the cooperation of its members, it can be all it was meant to be. We can truly become a global community."

"Can you briefly outline that in a few seconds?"

Carpathia's laugh appeared deep and genuine. "That is always dangerous," he said, "but I will try. As you know, the Security Council of the United Nations has five permanent members: the United States, the Russian Federation, Britain, France, and China. I propose choosing another five, just one each from the five different regions of the world. Then you would have ten permanent members of the Security Council, but the rest of my plan is revolutionary. Currently the five permanent members have veto power. Votes on procedure require a nine-vote majority; votes on substance require a majority, including all five permanent members. I propose a tougher system. I proposed unanimity."

"I beg your pardon?"

"Select carefully the representative ten permanent members. They must get input from and support from all the countries in their respective regions."

"It sounds like a nightmare."

"But it would work, and here is why. A nightmare is what happened to us last week. The time is right for the peoples of the world to rise up and insist that their governments disarm and destroy all but ten percent of their weapons. That ten percent would be, in effect, donated to the United Nations so it could return to its rightful place as a global peacekeeping body, with the authority and power in the equipment to do the job."

Bruce paused the tape yet again and apologized to the kids. "I'm sorry to make you listen to all that discussing of the ins and outs of the United Nations, but I think you can catch the drift there. Does anyone hear anything that sounds suspicious, based on what we've been studying in the book of Revelation?"

Judd took a breath to speak, but Vicki beat him to the punch. "There's all kinds of stuff in Revelation about the ten kings! You think Carpathia's idea of ten rulers matches up with that?"

"What do you think?" Bruce said.

"I guess it's pretty hard to argue with," Vicki said.

"Let me just play another couple of moments from this tape, which I find more than alarming." Bruce started the tape.

"What is your personal goal?" Theodore was asking. "A leadership role in the European Common Market?"

"Romania is not even a member, as you know. But no, I have no personal goal of leadership, except as a voice. We must disarm, we must empower the United Nations, we must move to one currency, and we must become a global village."

Bruce turned the tape off and removed it from the VCR. "Would you believe that several adults who have talked to me found Nicolae Carpathia a very impressive guy?"

"That doesn't surprise me at all," Vicki said. "He's a *very* impressive guy. He seems so sincere and humble."

"If this man is the Antichrist," Bruce said, "he will be attractive, charming, and a great deceiver. Of course, if he were for real, he would also be attractive and charming. We must be, as the Bible says, wise as serpents and gentle as doves as we study this. But think with me for a moment. If this man is the Antichrist—and we already know that since these tapes were recorded he has been installed as secretary-general of the U.N.—think what the world is doing if it does what he says."

The kids sat silent for a moment. Judd looked at the others. They looked puzzled. He had already thought of it. "He calls himself a pacifist," Judd said. "But what if he's not? What if he's a dictator? He's talked everyone else into giving up their weapons, destroying most of them and giving the rest to him. He'll have all the firepower. We'd better *hope* he's a pacifist!"

Bruce nodded. "Now let me show you this tape I recorded from CNN. It was shot in Israel, and it's the strangest report. What you'll see first is a mob in front of the famous Wailing Wall in Jerusalem. They're

surrounding two men who seem to be shouting. Watch and listen."

"No one knows the two men," said the
CNN reporter on the scene, "who refer to
each other as Eli and Moishe. They have
stood here before the Wailing Wall since just
before dawn, preaching in a style frankly
reminiscent of the old American evangelists.
Of course, the Orthodox Jews here are in an
uproar, charging the two with desecrating
this holy place by proclaiming that Jesus
Christ of the New Testament is the fulfill-
ment of the Torah's prophecy of a messiah.

"Thus far there has been no violence,
though tempers are flaring, and authorities
keep a watchful eye. Israeli police and mili-
tary personnel have always been loath to
enter this area, leaving religious zealots here
to handle their own problems. This is the
most explosive situation in the Holy Land
since the destruction of the Russian air force,
and this newly prosperous nation has been
concerned almost primarily with outside
threats.

"For CNN, this is Dan Bennett in Jerusalem."

Judd noticed Bruce was particularly excited
now. "I know you've already seen some of
these reports, but you must recognize those
two men preaching at the Wailing Wall as

the two witnesses prophesied in Scripture.
The Bible says that those two men will be
safe from harm and will have power over
even the rainfall in Israel for the first half of
the Tribulation period. They have the power
to keep it from raining, the power to turn
water into blood, and the power to breathe
fire on people who try to harm them before
the due time. What will be really incredible is
that when they are finally assassinated, the
Scripture says they will lie in the street for
three days before the eyes of the entire world.
Before technology as we know it, most bibli-
cal experts considered this to be figurative or
symbolic language. How could the whole
world see two men lying in the streets for
three days? Well, now we know. Most will
likely watch this on CNN.

"The people who have hated these two
men will wildly celebrate their deaths. But
after three days, God will audibly call them
into heaven by simply saying, 'Come up
here.'"

Lionel leaned forward and shook his head,
laughing. "That ought to change a few minds
real quick!"

"Remember what I said about God raising
up 144,000 Jews who would believe in
Christ and begin to evangelize around the

world?" Bruce said. "I believe these two will be leading the way."

Bruce turned the tape on again. A CNN anchorwoman had turned to national news. "New York is still abuzz following several appearances today by new Romanian president Nicolae Carpathia. The thirty-three-year-old leader wowed the media at a small press conference this morning, followed by a masterful speech to the United Nations General Assembly in which he had the entire crowd standing and cheering, including the press. Associates of Carpathia have announced that he has already extended his schedule to include addresses to several international meetings in New York over the next two weeks and that he has been invited by President Fitzhugh to speak to a joint session of Congress and spend a night at the White House.

"At a press conference this afternoon the president voiced support for the new leader."

The president's image filled the screen. He said, "At this difficult hour in world history, it's crucial that lovers of peace and unity step forward to remind us that we're part of the global community. Any friend of peace is a friend of the United States, and Mr. Carpathia is a friend of peace."

CNN broadcast a question asked of the

president. "Sir, what do you think of Carpathia's ideas for the U.N.?"

"Let me just say this: I don't believe I've ever heard anybody, inside or outside the U.N., show such a total grasp of the history and organization and direction of the place. He's done his homework, and he has a plan. I was listening. I hope the respective ambassadors and Secretary-General Ngumo were, too. No one should see a fresh vision as a threat. I'm sure every leader in the world shares my view that we need all the help we can get at this hour."

The anchorwoman continued: "Out of New York late this evening comes a report that a *Global Weekly* writer has been cleared of all charges and suspicion in the death of a Scotland Yard investigator. Cameron Williams, award-winning senior writer at the *Weekly*, had been feared dead in a car bombing that took the life of the investigator, Alan Tompkins, who was also an acquaintance of Williams."

"I need to tell you about this young man, Williams," Bruce said.

"I know who he is," Lionel said. "He called me on the phone once, looking for my mother."

"And he was on the plane with me the night of the Rapture," Judd said.

"Well," Bruce said, "he's a friend of Captain Steele, and he has spoken directly to Carpathia. He says Carpathia told him that Israel needs protection the United Nations can provide. Israel has a formula that makes the desert bloom. In exchange for that formula, Carpathia says the world will be content to grant them peace. If the other nations disarm and surrender a tenth of their weapons to the U.N., only the U.N. will have to sign a peace accord with Israel. If Cameron Williams is right, the agreement with Israel, in my mind, would signal the start of the seven-year tribulation period.

"Our time is up for this evening, but next time I want to start teaching you what I have been teaching a small adult group. I have drawn out a time line from several different sources that should give us a rough outline of what to expect during this, the most difficult period that will ever be recorded in the annals of time."

Judd, for one, couldn't wait to return and learn more. As he drove home that night, he could hardly get a word in edgewise. The other three were chattering away about what they had heard from Bruce. Finally, Ryan said, "Judd, what do you think Bruce expects us to do with all this stuff? I mean, we can't go to New York and fight this Carpathia guy, can we?"

"Of course not," Judd said. "I think Bruce just believes we'll be better off knowing our enemy than not knowing him. Our job is to bring as many people to Christ as possible over the next seven years, and you know that's not going to make us popular with any of God's enemies, especially the Antichrist."

NINE

Now What?

THE next morning, Judd had two problems on his mind, and they both had to do with females. He had wrestled in the night with an idea for Talia Grey. And just after he thought he had the perfect plan to bounce off Bruce, he was awakened by the telephone.

Of all things, the call came from inside the house. Judd's father had had two phone lines, so he could run his computer and fax machine when he worked at home. "I'm sorry to bother you, Judd," Vicki said, and it was obvious to him that she was crying.

Judd rolled up on one elbow and cradled the phone while glancing at the alarm clock. It was after three in the morning. He had just dozed off after coming up with his Talia Grey idea. "It's no bother, Vicki," he said. "What's up?"

"I was just wondering if I could talk to you for a while?"

"Sure. You mean on the phone right now, or . . . ?"

"I thought maybe face-to-face, like in the kitchen. That is if you think it would be OK."

"Is it an emergency, Vicki?"

"No," she said sadly. "I guess it can wait until tomorrow."

"No!" he said. "If it was worth calling in the middle of the night, it's worth talking about now. I'll meet you in five minutes."

Judd changed into jeans and a sweatshirt, splashed cold water on his face, and headed down to the kitchen.

A few minutes later he and Vicki sat sipping milk while she unburdened herself. "I just feel guilty, I guess," she said. "I mean, I love Bruce just like we all do, and his arguments are really convincing."

"I'm not following you," Judd said. "What is it you're feeling guilty about?"

"I don't believe him, that's all!" she blurted.

"Don't believe him about what?"

"The Antichrist!"

Judd slid his chair back and looked at her, brows raised. "After all Bruce has told us and explained to us about prophecy and the characteristics of the Antichrist, you don't think Nicolae Carpathia is the guy?"

Vicki was fighting tears. "Don't put me down about it, Judd, please!"

"I'm not! I'm just stunned. Tell me why."

"I don't know, and I'm afraid to tell Bruce. I see this Carpathia guy on TV, and he's so charming and smooth and convincing—I guess I'm one of the deceived. I can't seem to get into my mind that he's a bad guy."

"You know what Bruce would say, Vicki. He would say that that alone almost proves that Carpathia *is* the Antichrist."

Vicki nodded miserably. "I know," she said. "I feel like such a fool. But I can't just decide something is true only because the people I know and love and respect say it is. I want to agree with Bruce and all of you, but that's why I feel so guilty. I guess I need to be convinced."

"Are you looking to me to convince you? It's true I agree with Bruce on this, but I'm no more of a student of it than you are. If Bruce can't convince you, I sure can't."

"I know," Vicki said. "I guess what I'm looking for is just some sympathy and someone to talk to."

"I can do that," Judd said. "But what do you think it will take to convince you?"

"I don't know, but I sure wouldn't mind talking to that *Global Weekly* writer."

"Cameron Williams?"

"Yes."

"I thought he was based in New York," Judd said, "but he must have been around here. He talked to Bruce, and Bruce says he's a friend of the Steeles."

"If he has actually talked to Carpathia," Vicki said, "I think it would be fantastic for him to come and talk to us. In fact, I think it would be great if he came and talked to the whole church."

"Slow down there, Vicki. Bruce hasn't even said whether or not Williams is a Christian. And if he is, he sure can't be talking about Carpathia in public, especially if he believes Carpathia is the Antichrist."

Vicki slumped in the kitchen chair, her arms folded. She looked down. "I know," she whispered.

"But, hey, it sure wouldn't hurt to ask Bruce about him. You want me to?"

"I can ask him myself," Vicki said. "I just don't want to tell Bruce yet that I am not convinced about Carpathia."

Judd rinsed their glasses in the sink. He turned and looked expectantly at Vicki, who still sat there, staring at the floor. "You think I'm awful?" she asked.

"Hardly," he said. "The truth is, I think you're pretty special."

She looked up at him shyly. "I wasn't looking for a compliment," she said. "But I appreciate that."

Judd had not planned to say anything like that, and he had nothing to follow it with. "I'm good at keeping secrets," he said, "if that means anything to you."

"Of course it does, Judd. It means a lot to me that I can talk to you without the fear of being quoted."

Judd had trouble getting back to sleep, and early in the morning he felt the need to talk directly with Bruce. He would not betray Vicki's confidence, but he agreed that getting a chance to meet Cameron Williams would be a great thing for him and his friends. Also, he wanted to talk about his idea for Talia Grey.

When Judd called, Bruce told him he had another appointment in half an hour, but that he could see Judd right away, if he was available. "If I'm available?" Judd said. "It seems all I have is time. If they don't reopen our high school soon, what else am I going to do but talk to you?"

"Frankly, Judd," Bruce said, "time is something I wish I had more of."

Judd hurried to the church. Bruce's secretary, Loretta, ushered him into Bruce's office, where he found Bruce hunched over his Bible and several commentaries. "I know you don't have much time, so let me get right to it. I was wondering if you've already found a lawyer to help Talia Grey."

"As a matter of fact, I have. That's my next appointment."

"I don't suppose it would be possible for me to talk to him."

"Sure it would. Why not? But why are you assuming it's a *him*?"

"Oh, it's not?"

"Her name is Beth Murray. If you can hang around, you'll meet her in a few minutes. What else was on your mind?"

"This one might be tougher, Bruce. When you said you spoke with Cameron Williams, was that on the phone, or was he at the church here?"

"He was here," Bruce said. Bruce sat studying Judd, his eyes narrowing. "Why do you ask?"

"Is he a Christian?"

"As a matter of fact, he is. And he just happens to have one of the most incredible stories I've ever heard. The only problem is, I'm not sure he's at liberty to share it widely."

"Will he be back? Would he be able to meet with us? I think we'd all love to hear his

experiences, especially if he's actually talked
with Carpathia."

"Let me think about this for a minute,"
Bruce said. He stood, turned his back, and
strode to the window. He peered into the
parking lot for several seconds. When he
turned back to face Judd, he appeared to
have come to a decision. "You know what?"
he said. "This is going to be totally up to Mr.
Williams, of course, but I think I'm going to
give the Junior Tribulation Force the true
test."

"I hope you know I have no idea what
you're talking about," Judd said.

Bruce sat on the edge of his desk and
looked down kindly at Judd. "It just so happens that Cameron Williams has been reas-
signed to Chicago. He had been headquartered in New York for several years, but
he will be living in this area now for a
while."

"And he'll be coming to this church?"

Bruce nodded. "He's become the fourth
member of the Tribulation Force, along with
the Steeles and me."

"And what's this about some sort of a
test?"

"Yes, a true test for you kids."

"By the way, Bruce, we don't mind being
referred to as kids, because that's what we

are. But I don't think any of us would be excited about the term *Junior Tribulation Force*, or whatever."

"Sorry. It's just that your adult counterparts, the four people who make up the inner core of serious Bible students here, as I've told you, refer to themselves as the Tribulation Force."

"Call us the Kids Tribulation Force then," Judd suggested.

"Fair enough," Bruce said.

"And this big test . . . ?"

"No promises now," Bruce cautioned, "but I think I'm going to ask Cameron Williams to tell you kids his story. The reason I call that a big test is that if you are going to be called the younger version of the Tribulation Force, it requires keeping life-and-death secrets. Buck Williams—"

"Buck?"

"That's his nickname, yes. Buck Williams is privileged to have personal access to Nicolae Carpathia himself. As a new Christian, that puts him in a very dangerous situation. All I can do is ask him to tell you his story. If he chooses not to, we'll all have to accept that. If, however, he does decide to entrust you with the story, it must never be repeated to anyone anywhere without Buck's express permission. Is that understood?"

Judd nodded, his pulse quickening. *What in the world might the story be?* "Can I ask you something else, Bruce?"

"Of course."

"You did say that Williams believes Nicolae Carpathia is the Antichrist?"

"The fact is, Judd, Buck believed Nicolae Carpathia was the Antichrist even before Buck became a believer. In fact, I believe his coming to that conclusion helped persuade Buck to come to Christ."

"Wow! Do you think Buck would have any trouble convincing someone that Carpathia is the Antichrist?"

"Absolutely none," Bruce said. "Why? You know someone who needs convincing?"

"I didn't say that."

"But I asked you that."

"Let's just say I could use some more convincing myself," Judd said. "It seems this is an important enough deal that we should all be very sure about it. You have to admit, we could sure use somebody like Carpathia, I mean if he was for real."

"He appears as an angel of light," Bruce said, sighing. "Don't ever forget that."

Loretta poked her head into Bruce's office. "Excuse me, gentlemen," she said. "Pastor Barnes, your next appointment is here."

TEN

Facing the Future

JUDD appreciated Bruce's custom of having strangers tell their stories immediately after being introduced. Everyone now attending New Hope had, of course, been left behind at the Rapture, and so each had a story to tell. Where were they when it happened? How had they missed out? Whom had they lost? How did they find the truth? And what were they doing now?

The lawyer, Beth Murray, was an extremely tall, dark-haired woman with sharp features but a soft smile. When she and Bruce and Judd were seated, Bruce asked Judd to tell his story first. As many times as he had told it, it never grew old for him. There were sad parts, of course. Regrets. Fear. Even terror. There were parts he didn't much enjoy rehashing—discovering his family was gone, realizing he was alone in the world.

And yet Judd loved to get to the grace part. He never grew tired of telling the wonderful news that he had been given a second chance. God's grace extended to him despite his rebellion and failure the first time around. He realized he had been more than fortunate. He could easily have been killed in an accident during the Rapture, as so many others had. His voice grew quavery when he told how he had learned from Bruce that the Christian life was a series of new beginnings.

Judd became quickly aware that Beth Murray had learned well the listening part of her craft. She leaned forward, rested her chin on her fist, and locked in to his gaze. She made him feel as if he were the most important person in her world just then. It seemed she didn't want to miss a word. It nearly made Judd uncomfortable, but soon he realized it was her way of encouraging him, and he plunged ahead.

Ms. Murray grew emotional along with Judd as he recounted how he had met the other three kids and had invited them to live with him. She particularly enjoyed the brief stories of how each had come to Christ. "I can't wait to meet each of them and hear them tell of their own journeys."

Her story was a new one to Judd. She said she had been an atheist, "but in actuality, describing myself as an agnostic would have been more precise. I worshiped at the altar of education, achievement, and materialism. I married a nonpracticing Jewish man ten years ago, and we got along fine until about eighteen months ago. I believed I was the most open-minded and tolerant person in the world until Isaiah converted to Christianity and began attending a messianic synagogue. I was mortified. I was angry. I refused to discuss it. I would not attend with him. Our marriage was nearly on the rocks, and yet I could not deny the change in him. No matter how I treated him, he loved me and forgave me and treated me kindly.

"I was not happy in a marriage with a man I respected but whose belief system I could not respect. Much as I love children, I'm so grateful Isaiah and I decided not to have any. I was on the brink of an affair when the Rapture occurred. Isaiah had warned me of that, and so I was speeding toward that messianic synagogue within ten minutes of the disappearances. No one was there. Every person associated with that fellowship was gone. I stumbled across New Hope. I simply drove past and saw it here, a church with a few people milling about. I met Pastor Barnes, I watched the videotape that had been prepared for people just like me, and I joined the kingdom."

With their stories—which Bruce sometimes referred to as "testimonies"—out of the way, they got down to the reason for their meeting. Beth Murray told Judd that Bruce had brought her up-to-date on Talia Grey's case. "I have studied her file, and it doesn't look good for her at this point. She was much more deeply involved than you might have assumed in many of the crimes committed by her brother and his friend. The best thing we have going for us is that court dockets are jammed and only getting worse. I have a few ideas, but Bruce tells me you have one too."

"If you don't mind," Judd said.

"Let's hear it," she said.

Judd told her of the idea that had come to him in the middle of the night. "I don't claim to know much about the law, and I guess I thought of this because of the things I've seen on TV. But I was just wondering whether she might be able to help herself by agreeing to testify against LeRoy and Cornelius."

"That's an excellent idea, Judd," she said. "I had been thinking of something along those lines as well. If she is willing and brave enough to withstand the threats of LeRoy's and her brother's associates, she just may be able to do herself lot of good. Good thinking."

"Actually," Judd said, "now that I have met you and think about it a little, I see one more big advantage to having you working with Talia."

"And what's that?" Ms. Murray said.

"You'll have to interview Sergeant Tom Fogarty, won't you?"

"Yes. In fact, I already have."

"And did you meet his wife?"

"Just briefly. It was long enough, however, for me to sense that there's some tension there."

Judd and Bruce filled her in, and the three of them agreed to be praying for just the right opening for Beth to support Mrs. Fogarty in her new faith and to perhaps reach Tom for Christ.

Judd drove home that day feeling better than he had in a long time. He was glad he had met Beth Murray, and he was optimistic about the futures of his new acquaintances. He knew there were no guarantees. He knew that in real life, not everyone made decisions or took the actions one might want them to.

He enjoyed being able to tell Vicki that he
had not only kept her confidence but that
she would also get her wish to meet Cameron Williams and hear of his experiences
with Nicolae Carpathia. That meeting came
one momentous afternoon the following
week, when Mr. Williams was able to get
away from the Chicago bureau office of
Global Weekly magazine and join the Kids
Tribulation Force and Bruce for a highly
secret meeting.

To Vicki, the ruggedly handsome thirtyish
Buck Williams seemed like a man more com-
fortable with adults than with teenagers. He
greeted them warmly enough, but he was a
bit formal and quiet, something she knew he
couldn't be normally with a job like his. He
joined them in their prayer time, but then he
sat behind the kids.

Bruce began the meeting by finishing his
promised lesson on the time chart of the
seven-year tribulation. "It looks to me," he
said, "and to many of the experts who came
before us, like this period of history we're in
right now will last for the first twenty-one
months of the Tribulation. They encompass

what the Bible calls the seven Seal Judgments, or the judgments of the seven-sealed
scroll. Then comes another twenty-one-
month period in which we will see the seven
Trumpet Judgments. In the last forty-two
months of the seven years, if we have sur-
vived, we will endure the most severe test,
the seven Vial Judgments. The last half of the
seven years is called the Great Tribulation,
and if we are alive at the end of it, we will be
rewarded by seeing the glorious appearing of
Christ.

"These judgments get progressively worse,
and they will be harder and harder to survive. If we die, we will be in heaven with
Christ and our loved ones. But we may suffer
horrible deaths. If we somehow make it
through the seven terrible years, especially
the last half, the Glorious Appearing will be
all that more glorious. Christ will come back
to set up his thousand-year reign on Earth,
the Millennium.

"Let me just briefly outline the seven-
sealed scroll from Revelation 5 and 6, and
then we'll hear from Mr. Williams. On the
one hand, I don't want to give you a spirit of
fear, but we all know we're still here because
we neglected salvation before the Rapture. I
know we're all grateful for the second

chance, but we cannot expect to escape the trials that are coming."

Bruce explained that the first four seals in this scroll were described as men on four horses: a white horse, a red horse, a black horse, and a pale horse. "The white horseman apparently is the Antichrist, who ushers in one to three months of diplomacy while getting organized and promising peace.

"The red horse signifies war. Three rulers from the south will oppose the Antichrist, and millions will be killed."

Bruce turned a sheet on his flip chart. "All that killing will likely come within the next eighteen months. Immediately following that, which will take only three to six months because of the nuclear weaponry available, the Bible predicts inflation and famine—the black horse. As the rich get richer, the poor starve to death. More millions will die that way. Sad to say, it gets worse. That killer famine could be as short as two or three months before the arrival of the fourth Seal Judgment, the fourth horseman on a pale horse—the symbol of death. Besides the postwar famine, a plague will sweep the entire world. Before the fifth Seal Judgment a quarter of the world's current population will be dead. You're going to recognize this judgment, because we've talked about it before.

Remember my telling you about 144,000 Jewish witnesses who evangelize the world for Christ? The world leader and the harlot, which is the name for the one-world religion that denies Christ, will murder many of the converts, perhaps millions.

"The sixth Seal Judgment consists of God pouring out his wrath against the killing of his saints. This will come in the form of a worldwide earthquake so devastating that no instruments will be able to measure it. It will be so bad that people will cry out for rocks to fall on them and put them out of their misery. The seventh seal introduces the seven Trumpet Judgments, which will take place in the second quarter of the seven years. That's the second twenty-one months."

Bruce concluded, "Most believers will be murdered or die from war, famine, plagues, or earthquakes."

Vicki was depressed. She found herself actually looking forward to Mr. Williams's presentation. She knew times would be rough, and she didn't expect any better. But this was devastating. Whatever Cameron Williams had to say had to be better than this.

"First," Mr. Williams said, "I go by *Buck*. Calling me *Mr. Williams* makes me feel too old, and calling me *Cameron* makes me think you're making fun of me the way kids did in grade school years ago."

Vicki couldn't help but smile. There wasn't much to smile about these days, but Buck Williams's rapid-fire delivery was fun to listen to. Her mind had been changed about him immediately. He proved to be an intense, impassioned guy. And he was a natural-born teacher.

"Remember your vow of confidentiality," Buck said, "and here we go. My assignment, as I understand it, is to use my own experience and conversations with Nicolae Carpathia to convince you he is who Bruce fears he is. Let me run this down quickly. As you may have seen on the news, he's asked for resolutions from the U.N. supporting some of the things he wants to do. These include a seven-year peace treaty with Israel in exchange for his ability to broker the desert-fertilizer formula. He's moving the U.N. to New Babylon. He's establishing a one-world religion, probably headquartered in Italy. Though he might have trouble with the Jews on that one, he has promised to help them rebuild their temple during the years of the peace treaty. He believes they deserve special treatment. All those things are predicted in the Bible."

Buck Williams had been standing. Now he

pulled up a chair and sat with the kids. "Let me tell you a story that I wouldn't believe myself if I had not lived it. I have gained the attention and respect of Nicolae Carpathia. My former boss has become his public relations man. Because of that, I got invited to a private meeting at the U.N. immediately before Carpathia was to introduce to the world his ten new international ambassadors.

"I knew well the characteristics of the Antichrist, mostly based on a lengthy conversation I'd had with Bruce. I was not at that time a believer. When I got to Carpathia's private meeting, I felt such an intense presence of evil and foreboding that I hurried from the room and got alone where I could receive Christ. I went back to the meeting, where I witnessed something so astounding that, had I not received Christ and he had not been in control of my mind and spirit, I know I would have been brainwashed like everyone else in that room.

"You heard what happened there. The world, the press—in fact, everyone else in that room that day except Nicolae Carpathia and me—believe that one of those ambassadors grabbed a security guard's gun and shot himself. In the process he killed Carpathia's biggest supporter."

Yes, Vicki thought, *that's exactly the way we've heard it happened.* "Not true?" she asked.

"Not true at all. After Carpathia went around the room, shaking hands and welcoming each new ambassador to his team, he borrowed a huge, powerful handgun from the guard and asked his financial supporter, a man named Jonathan Stonagal, to kneel before him.

"Stonagal did not want to do it. He was humiliated at the request. Carpathia pleaded with him to trust him, calling him his best friend in the world. Once Stonagal was on his knees, Carpathia was in no hurry. He spoke calmly and quietly, and I will remember every word he said for as long as I live. He said, 'I am going to kill Mr. Stonagal with a painless hollow-point round to the brain, which he will neither hear nor feel. The rest of us will experience some ringing in our ears. This will be instructive for you all. You will understand cognitively that I am in charge, that I fear no man, and that no one can oppose me.'

"Carpathia went on to say, 'When Mr. Stonagal is dead, I will tell you what you will remember. And lest anyone feel I have not been fair, let me not neglect to add that a high-velocity bullet at this range will also kill Mr. Todd-Cothran.'"

This is preposterous, Vicki thought. *How could anyone let a man get away with something like that?*

"I was so shocked and scared," Buck said, "I could not move.

"With his so-called dear friend kneeling there, Carpathia murdered both Stonagal and Todd-Cothran with one shot. I just stared, my mouth hanging open, as others pushed back from the table and covered their heads in fear. Carpathia placed the gun in Stonagal's limp right hand and twisted his finger around the trigger. Carpathia said kindly, as if speaking to children, 'What we have just witnessed here was a horrible, tragic end to two otherwise extravagantly productive lives. These men were two I respected and admired more than any others in the world. What compelled Mr. Stonagal to rush the guard, disarm him, take his own life and that of his British colleague, I do not know and may never fully understand.'

"Carpathia then went around the room, asking each person what he had seen. Every one of them told the story exactly the way Carpathia had described it. When he got to me, God told me to say nothing. Carpathia assumed I was speechless from shock or because he was controlling my mind. And I had no idea whether he knew or not that I knew the truth. When the police arrived and began taking eyewitness accounts, I rushed back to my office and began writing the story. My boss burst in and demanded to know why I had not been at the meeting. I could not convince him I had been there. No one I have talked to in the room remembers I was ever even there.

"You kids don't know me from Adam. You don't have to believe a word I say. But I swear to you as a new brother in Christ that this is the truth. Nicolae Carpathia is evil personified, and if he is not the Antichrist, I don't know who is."

Vicki knew the others were as impressed as she. Buck looked spent. Vicki knew what he had said had a ring of truth to it. She believed him instinctively. And she had the same thought the others had at the same time. As one, they reached out and gently touched Buck's shoulders. Then they knelt around him and prayed for him.

Judd, for one, was proud to be a part of this little group, in this church, under this pastor, and alongside people like Buck Williams. He and his friends were just kids to some people, but their task, just like that of the adult Tribulation Force, was clear. Their goal was nothing less than to stand against and fight the enemies of God during the seven most chaotic years the planet would ever see.

ABOUT THE AUTHORS

Jerry B. Jenkins (www.jerryjenkins.com) is the author of more than one hundred books. The former vice president for publishing for the Moody Bible Institute of Chicago, he also served many years as editor of *Moody* magazine. His writing has appeared in a variety of publications, including *Reader's Digest, Parade,* in-flight magazines, and many Christian periodicals. He writes books in four genres: biographies, marriage and family, fiction for children, and fiction for adults.

Jenkins's biographies include books with Hank Aaron, Bill Gaither, Luis Palau, Walter Payton, Orel Hershiser, Nolan Ryan, Brett Butler, and Billy Graham, among many others. The Hershiser, Ryan, and Graham books reached the *New York Times* best-seller list.

Four of his apocalyptic novels, coauthored with Tim LaHaye, *Left Behind, Tribulation Force, Nicolae,* and *Soul Harvest* have appeared on the Christian Booksellers Association's best-selling fiction list and the *Publishers Weekly* religion best-sellers list. *Left Behind* was nominated for Novel of the Year by the Evangelical Christian Publishers Association in both 1997 and 1998.

As a marriage and family author and speaker, Jenkins has been a frequent guest on Dr. James Dobson's *Focus on the Family* radio program.

Jerry is also the writer of the nationally syndicated sports story comic strip *Gil Thorp,* distributed to newspapers across the United States by Tribune Media Services.

Jerry and Dianna and their sons live in northeastern Illinois and in Colorado.

Speaking engagement bookings are available through speaking@jerryjenkins.com.

Tim LaHaye is a noted author, minister, counselor, and nationally recognized speaker on family life and Bible prophecy. He is the founder and president of Family Life Seminars and the founder of The PreTrib Research Center. Presently Dr. LaHaye speaks at many of the major Bible prophecy conferences in the U.S. and Canada, where his seven current prophecy books are very popular.

Dr. LaHaye is a graduate of Bob Jones University and holds an M.A. and Doctor of Ministry degree from Western Conservative Theological Seminary. For twenty-five years he pastored one of the nation's outstanding churches in San Diego, which grew to three locations. During that time he founded two accredited Christian high schools, a Christian school system of ten schools, and Christian Heritage College.

Dr. LaHaye has written over forty nonfiction titles, with over ten million copies in print in thirty-two languages. He has written books on a wide variety of subjects, such as family life, temperaments, and Bible prophecy. His current fiction works written with Jerry Jenkins, *Left Behind, Tribulation Force, Nicolae,* and *Soul Harvest,* have all reached number one on the Christian best-seller charts. Other works by Dr. LaHaye are *Spirit-Controlled Temperament; How to Be Happy though Married; Revelation, Illustrated and Made Plain;* and a youth fiction series, *Left Behind: The Kids.*

He is the husband of Beverly LaHaye, founder and chairperson of Concerned Women for America. Together they have four children and nine grandchildren. Snow skiing, waterskiing, motorcycling, golfing, vacationing with family, and jogging are among his leisure activities.

The Future Is Clear

In one shocking moment, millions around the globe disappear.
Those left behind face an uncertain future—especially the four
kids who now find themselves alone.

Best-selling authors Jerry B. Jenkins and
Tim LaHaye present the Rapture and
Tribulation through the eyes of four
friends—Judd, Vicki, Lionel, and Ryan.
As the world falls in around them, they
band together to find faith and fight
the evil forces that threaten their lives.

#1: The Vanishings Four friends
face Earth's last days together.

#2: Second Chance The kids
search for the truth.

#3: Through the Flames The
kids risk their lives.

#4: Facing the Future The kids
prepare for battle.

#5: Nicolae High The Young Trib
Force goes back to school.

#6: The Underground The Young Trib Force fights back.

BOOKS #7 AND #8 COMING SOON!

Discover the latest about the Left Behind series and complete line of products at

www.leftbehind.com